Louis Becke, Walter Jeffrey

A First Fleet Family

A Hitherto Unpublished Narrative of Certain Remarkable Adventures

Louis Becke, Walter Jeffrey

A First Fleet Family
A Hitherto Unpublished Narrative of Certain Remarkable Adventures

ISBN/EAN: 9783337111854

Printed in Europe, USA, Canada, Australia, Japan

Cover: Foto ©Andreas Hilbeck / pixelio.de

More available books at **www.hansebooks.com**

A FIRST FLEET FAMILY

WORKS BY LOUIS BECKE

———◆———

THE EBBING OF THE TIDE: South Sea Stories. Large
    Crown 8vo, Cloth, 6s.

BY REEF AND PALM (*Autonym Library*). Preface by the
    EARL OF PEMBROKE. Third Edition. Paper, 1s. 6d. ;
    Cloth, 2s

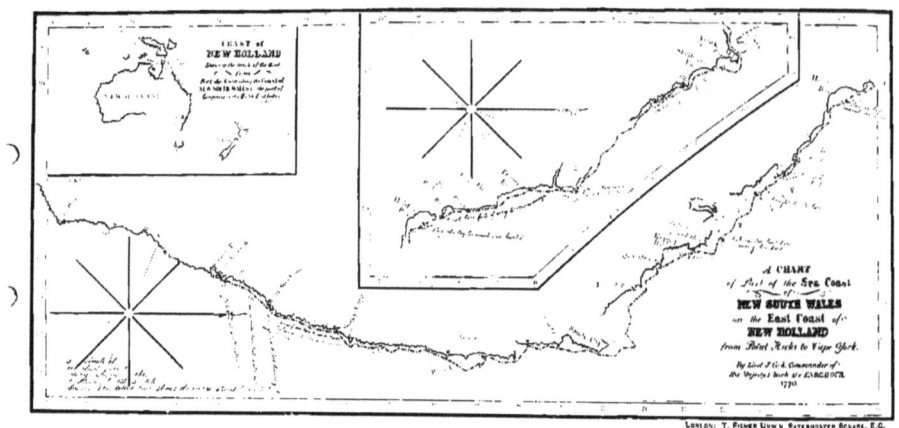

A FIRST FLEET FAMILY.

A HITHERTO UNPUBLISHED
NARRATIVE OF CERTAIN
REMARKABLE ADVENTURES
COMPILED FROM THE PAPERS
OF SERGEANT WILLIAM DEW
OF THE MARINES

BY

LOUIS BECKE

AND

WALTER JEFFERY

London

T. FISHER UNWIN

PATERNOSTER SQUARE

MDCCCXCVI.

PREFACE

THE Editors of this narrative, some months since, received from Mr W. J. Dew the journals of his grandfather, Sergeant Dew, with the request that if they were likely to be of interest to the public, the Editors would put them into the form of a book and have them published.

The papers were submitted to the Editors, whose names appear with this work, on the ground that one of them is a personal friend of the present Dew family, and both of them are well acquainted with the localities and the events referred to by the Sergeant.

Sergeant Dew, before his death, left instructions that should his descendants at any time determine to make public his remarkable narrative, everything that could possibly cause pain to any person living might be withheld from the printer.

As a matter of fact, the Editors found nothing in the papers the publication of which could cause anyone a moment's feeling of annoyance ; but any attempt made now to disguise the principal characters in the story would be futile, for the New South Wales Government has published, in a work called *The Historical Records of New South Wales*, nearly every fact here related.

In fact, a short account of the Bryants' escape —so far as the official knowledge of it goes— is to be found in most of the so-called histories of the Colony.

This being the case, the Editors determined to give the narrative as it stood, with only one reservation, and that is in the case of the name of Fairfax, which name is a fictitious one ; for the family whose ancestor was the officer who is known in the book under this name, might possibly object to being thus brought before the public. Some slight alterations have also been made in the English portion of the narrative in order to disguise the exact locality of the early scenes in Mr Dew's life.

It is only fair to the Editors to reproduce here a part of Mr Dew's letter, written by him, after reading the MS. of the work :—

'You have performed your task in a manner very gratifying to me. I quite agree with your change of ——'s name to Fairfax, and with your change of locality. I see you have corrected some of my grandfather's English and spelling. He was a little weak in the last particular, and some of his English would, of course, be too much out of date in these days of foreign words.—I am, yours gratefully,

W. J. DEW.'

The Editors express their indebtedness to the Historical Records above mentioned, and to Mr Barton's volumes in particular, for much information which enabled them to verify facts and dates in this narrative. The conspicuous ability of Mr Barton's work has enabled them to gain a knowledge of Phillip and his principal officers that, taken with Sergeant Dew's papers, has portrayed to their minds a vivid picture of the men. The necessity for curtailment, and the lack of ability on the part of the Editors, are the excuses offered to the reader, if he, when he has read this book, has not a fair idea of what manner of men they were. *The Historical Records of New South Wales* are largely indebted to

Philip Gidley King, Esq., M.L.C., of New South Wales, for much of what is published in them relating to King. The present Mr King is a grandson of Lieutenant King, and he very generously presented his country with many of his grandfather's papers. These documents have been of great use in preparing Mr Dew's narrative. Much that is purely history in Sergeant Dew's Journal has been of necessity omitted from this narrative ; but if sufficient interest is taken by the public in what is here printed, plenty of material is contained in the Dew papers to make another book of the Sergeant's early adventures, in which the matters related would bring to light many things never before published.

Sir Henry Parkes, while this was being prepared for the press, was severely attacked by certain 'patriotic' members of the New South Wales Assembly for having ordered from England a statue of Phillip, to be erected in Sydney.

It may appear strange to English readers that while there is more than one statue of Cook in Sydney, it is scarcely known to the majority of the Australian people that Phillip was the man

who founded their country and that Cook was
never inside the Heads of Port Jackson.

The school histories of the Colony are be-
neath notice, and the few men who have written
anything of the country's early days, such as
Bonwick, Bennett, or Barton, are never read.
It is safe to say that not one man in a thousand
i as the remotest idea of the early history of
New South Wales, beyond the fact that a
number of convicts were transported to it
something over a hundred years ago. Great
injustice has been done to the early founders
of the Colony by forgetting them; greater
injustice still is too often done to them when
they are remembered. For what has hitherto
been written and read about the very early
days has been, with few exceptions, stories
depicting the cruelties of the punishments in-
flicted upon the convicts. The felons have
always been the heroes and the authorities the
villains of the piece. Nearly everyone who has
written has followed the lead of Marcus Clarke.
The result is that his powerful novel, and true
enough picture of one side of the case—*His
Natural Life*—has been the only point of view
most readers are acquainted with. As a con-

sequence, the men have been mistakenly blamed
for the errors of the system, and no allowance
has been made for the times in which the events
described took place.   A maudlin sympathy
with the convicts has become the only impres-
sion too many people have of the times ; they
have no thought for such men as Phillip and
King, whose great hearts conquered the prejudices of their times and strove to look upon
their duties as less those of gaolers than
reformers.   And, above all, everyone seems
nowadays to have overlooked the fact that
the men who came prisoners to this country in
the very early days were, for the most part,
criminals who had forfeited their lives to their
country's laws.   In a word, they had, as they
put it among the class from which they were
drawn, 'got into trouble,' and we are apt, so
great is our sympathy for these prisoners, to
forget that no one asked them to do so.   For
it was only the ancestors of persons now living
who were sent out for poaching and political
crimes and such like trifles.   Everyone who
knows Australia must have learned that all the
convicts who are remembered by people at this
end of the century were really quite decent

people ; the records show that those who came in the last century were generally the worst of felons.

If this narrative of a man who lived among these people, and saw them as it were from two points of view, does not enable readers to look at both sides, as Sergeant Dew did, and if the story lacks interest, it is not the fault of Sergeant Dew's journal.

THE EDITORS.

SYDNEY, *June*, 1895.

CONTENTS

CHAPTER I

CONTENTS

CONTENTS XV

CONTENTS

A FIRST FLEET FAMILY

CHAPTER I

SOLCOMBE

To you, my dear children, who have as yet experienced
no privations and know not the true dreadfulness of a
life of great hardship, I leave this record of your father's
early career. May it serve to bring to your minds,
when those about you too readily judge harshly of
their fellow-men, that all, even the humblest and
poorest, may, if they steadily do their duty, rise to a
comfortable station in life and win the respect of those
whose respect is worth the winning.

That you may be able to follow your father's
fortunes from his earliest youth down to that happy
time when he was able to return from his foreign
adventures and settle, a prosperous man, in his native
country, I have added to my diary such particulars
as my now failing memory and the recollections of my
old comrades supply me with.

A

In the old family Bible which, as children has so often afforded you, with its pictures, a pleasant and proper Sunday afternoon's entertainment, you will find on that leaf where your names are written this entry :—

'William Dew, born February 28, 1764.'

It would be no good for me to pretend to be younger than I am, for, with the excellent schooling you have had, you could very easily cypher out my age. Your grandfather was a good, honest farmer, with a fine turn for smuggling—as who had not in our little village in those days? In truth, as is well known, smuggling was carried on among all conditions of people who lived on the English coast and in the Isle of Wight ; not only the fishermen but the small farmers, and even the big squires and landed gentry—some of whom held His Majesty's Commission of the Peace—had a hand in the contraband trade. Indeed, if all we hear be true, the art of landing a keg of good brandy under the noses of the Preventive Service is not yet lost upon the island.

Let me try and describe Solcombe as it was in those days, and you can see for yourselves if it has as much altered as the men and women are changed who live in it.

Solcombe—where some of you, as well as your father and grandfather, were born—lies at the back of the Wight, which is the side of the island nearest to the

French coast, and when I was a boy the farms there-about ran down almost to the water's edge—that is to say, to the ledges of the high chalk cliffs which formed a boundary wall and shut out the sea from sight, though in heavy weather its salt spray was flung high upward in drenching showers upon the gardens of the villagers. On a rough winter's night in the Channel, the roar of the breakers, as they smote the steep-to cliffs in all their unchecked fury, would shake the houses of the village, and strike terror to the hearts of those women in Solcombe—and there were many— who had their men-folk away at sea. Sometimes, especially when the force of the wind had broken a bit, the wild clamour of the beating surf could be heard half-way across to the other side of the island. Beating like this for ages against the cliffs, the sea had hollowed out of them many a dark and winding cavern, some of which ran far back into the very bowels of the land. And on both sides of Solcombe every little inlet and indentation on the coast-line gave a harbour to the smugglers for running their cargoes, and the natural caves provided glorious warehouses for French brandy and bales of fine silk and other gear sought after by grand ladies who cared but little that such things sometimes cost blood and death besides the money paid for them. In these caves the smuggled goods would remain till favourable opportunity came for either selling them on the island or sending them away across the Solent to where they would be quickly disposed of to people who lived by smuggling alone.

Difficult of access by land—save in rare cases—and familiar only to the dwellers in their near vicinity even by sea, these smugglers' storehouses were seldom discovered by the Preventive Service men ; but occasionally an informer would betray the intention of the smugglers to run a cargo, and then, perhaps, a desperate fight would follow, and more than one poor fellow would lose his life doing his duty, and a few prisoners would be manacled and gyved, and marched away and committed to Winchester Gaol.

George the Third was king in those days, and the war with the rebellious American colonists was looming up, though no one, as I have since heard, ever thought it would prove such a great and disastrous conflict as it did.

Father had a great notion of giving me some schooling, for he was something of a scholar himself, having in his young days been taught a good deal above his station ; and so I was kept at the village school till I grew to be quite a strapping fellow, and was full sixteen years of age.

The old schoolmaster had at one time been a soldier, and was always telling us boys about the doings at the wars. He had fought with Marlborough in more than one battle, and was very proud of a scar from a bayonet thrust through his leg. Sometimes, at the village inn, where the talk would turn upon the wars that were then going on, he would say to those present that, though it ill-becomed him at his age to boast, yet could he give them ocular demonstration that he had served his country and received honourable wounds ; and then, after some little coaxing, he would show the calf of his right leg, and condescend to drink a pint of ale with the company to the toast of 'God save His Majesty, and confusion to his enemies.'

Those were stirring times, for old England was fighting the Spaniards and the French and the Dutch, besides having on her hands the rebellion of the American colonies and the riots in London. And so it came about that, seeing my head had got stuffed full of silly notions of soldiering and going abroad to fight the king's battles, my father took me from school and set me to help on the farm, in the hope that in following the plough I should forget all about the glory of a red coat and white cross-belts and the rattle of the drum. My mother died just about that time. She was always ailing, and I am afraid that anxiety about me hastened her end, for she was terribly cut up at the way I was bitten with the craze for going a-soldiering.

Even now, after such long, long years, I can some-times see her face, so rough and wrinkled with care, yet so full of tenderness and love, as she clasped my hands in hers, with the death-shadows deepening upon her features, and a strange, yearning look in her fading eyes that brought a quick gush of tears to mine. Her last words to anyone on earth were spoken to me, for after she had, with failing strength, placed her hand upon my father's head as he knelt beside her, she turned to me and with her last breath murmured, 'And God keep you, my son.' Then she gave a long, heavy sigh and closed her eyes for ever.

After the shock of my mother's death had somewhat worn off, I turned again to my work upon the farm, but the only effect that following the plough had upon my mind was to make me continually ponder upon the subject of my wishes all the more. I was in great doubt as to which of two ways of serving the king and gratifying my inclinations was the shortest road to glory, whether it was better to go to sea and fight the Spaniards and French under such a man as Rodney, and return to my native village with a pocket full of prize money, or to seek honour and fortune with the land forces under our generals in the Americas.

CHAPTER II

MARY BROAD

THUS a year or two went by, and I grew less and less inclined to work honestly on the farm, and father grew more and more dissatisfied with me. Sometimes it was in my mind to take a boat over to Portsmouth and put myself in the way of the press-gangs, and thus get sent to sea in such a way that father would be made to believe that it was through no fault of mine; but yet, I thank God, I reflected that, whatever father might think, my conscience would give me no rest for acting such a lie.

It was about this time that Mary Broad became lady's-maid to Miss Fairfax, the daughter of the Squire of Solcombe, and I, foolish lad, fell in love with Mary the first time I saw her, and thus, with my love for going a-soldiering and love for her, my mind was in anything but a proper condition.

Squire Fairfax lived at Solcombe Manor House, and was the great man in that neighbourhood. He was a widower, with one son and one daughter, and

in appearance was a fine, portly man, with a keen,
blue eye and a face that showed his generous heart
and hasty temper.   The son, Charles Fairfax, was
a lieutenant in the Marines at the time that Mary
Broad went to live at the Manor House, and I
was very jealous of the effect his red coat and gold
lace would be likely to have upon the girl.

Mary's father was a young French officer who
had been taken prisoner and confined, with several
others, in Porchester Castle on the mainland.   He
was a lieutenant in a Breton regiment, and the
Solcombe folks, when he came to live among them,
much as they disliked foreigners, said he was a fine,
big, handsome man, and he quickly made friends
with the Solcombe people when he was released.
As he came of a Huguenot family, no one was surprised at a Solcombe girl falling in love with and
marrying him.   Yet, such is religious prejudice, that
when he died, soon after his daughter's birth, the
village folks said it was a judgment upon his wife
for marrying a man who, although a Protestant, was
yet a foreigner.   His proper name was not Broad,
but this is what his English neighbours made of it,
and so, after a time, the family were known as the
Broads, and Mary always wrote her name in this
way.   After her husband's death, Mary's mother
got a living by her needle, sewing for the fine
ladies who were friends of and visited the Fairfax
family, and contrived to give her daughter some

little education, as education went in those days. Then they came over and settled at Newport, and Mrs Broad opened a little shop, in which Mary served, and in which I used to spend a great deal of my pocket money, for no other reason than for the pleasure of being served by so fair and sweet-looking a young shop-woman.

Old as I am now, I have never forgotten her strangely handsome face and graceful figure. She was so different from the other young girls round about, that her manner, as well as her beauty, attracted notice. Her fatherw as, as I have said, a very hand-some man, and she had all his dark eyes and hair, and quick, short manner of speech, and even to Squire Fairfax she preserved a demeanour that, while not quite wanting in respect to such a gentleman, was yet by no means sufficiently humble and proper for one in her condition of life.

Miss Charlotte Fairfax was a spoilt young lady in those days, with a great will of her own, and her father was so bounden to her by his great affec-tion that she could do as she liked with him. One day, when she was in Newport, she went into Mrs Broad's shop to purchase some lace, or such-like women's fal-lal, and caught sight of Mary.

'Mercy me,' says she, 'what a pretty girl! And, pray, who are you, child? and where do you come from?'

Now, the word 'child' was not to Mary's liking,

for she tossed her head and gave no pleasant answer, although she knew who it was who spoke
to her. Then Mrs Broad stepped into the shop
and explained who they were, and the upshot of
it was that Mary went into service at the Manor
House as lady's-maid to Miss Charlotte, and in a
few weeks began to look more beautiful than ever,
by reason of the better garments that her mistress
clothed her with.

The Squire's daughter was then about two-and-
twenty years of age and Mary eighteen. The
young lady was a fair-haired and blue-eyed beauty,
with a great many silly notions in her head, and a
fine contempt for the country life she was leading,
and the few opportunities it afforded her to show
off the airs and graces she had learned from her
grand cousins who lived in London.

She soon made a confidant of Mary, and, indeed,
treated her more as a friend than a servant, and
I believe that Mary's natural resolution and serious,
determined nature soon dominated Miss Charlotte's
weaker character, and that in name only was pretty,
yellow-haired Miss Fairfax her mistress.

Indeed, 'twas this strong, determined nature of hers
that made Mary Broad go through so much future
misery with calm, unswerving fortitude for Will
Bryant—as you will see before I come to the end
of this journal.

The Bryants were well known in Solcombe,

although they lived a few miles from the village.
They came of Irish folk, and were not much liked
in the neighbourhood, for the Isle of Wighters
thought that the Bryants, being Irishers, must be
in secret sympathy with the French, and, as was
natural and proper, we hated the French in those
days, and were active in showing it, too.   Why,
I remember, long years afterwards, when there came
some fear of Bonaparte landing on the south coast
and conquering the country, and making us either
turn Papists or let our throats be cut, we formed
volunteer companies—that is, we served without pay
—to defend the island.   There is a story that one day
a poor monkey that some sailor had brought home
from foreign parts was given by him to an innkeeper
in payment for his score.   The creature escaped,
and was captured late at night somewhere near
Shanklin, by some ignorant rustics, and hanged in
the belief that the poor animal was a French spy.
Of course this story may not be true, and I have
my doubts about it ; but, however that may be, we
were very jealous in our hatred of the French, and,
indeed, of people who were suspected of having
sympathy with them, and the Isle of Wight rustics,
to the present day, are very ignorant.   Fortunately,
the Bryants were Protestants, and, by reason of
this, were not so much suspected and disliked as
they would have been had they been Papists, and
just at this particular time we did not happen to

be quite so bitter against the French, and had not the fear of Bonaparte attempting a landing as we had later on.

The Bryant family, father, mother and two sons, were either always smuggling or poaching, and the eldest son, William—the only one who has anything to do with this narrative—was the most notorious and daring smuggler on the island. He pretended to get his living as a waterman plying between Ryde and Portsmouth, but precious little work he did in that way. But—and this galled my jealous mind greatly —he had served a commission in a king's ship at one time, and had been one of a cutting-out party which captured a big French privateer belonging to St Malo, as she lay at anchor off the French coast. Many a yarn he would tell of his adventures, and this and his fine figure and great strength made him very popular with men and women both. And then, besides, he was a man ever free with his money, and I believe that this had much to do with the hold he gained upon the affections of Mary Broad.

One autumn afternoon in the year 1786, I was walking moodily along the ledge of one of the high cliffs, looking out seawards and thinking what I would give to be the captain of a frigate that was in sight bowling down Channel before a nine-knot breeze, when, as I turned my eyes landward again, I saw Mary coming towards me.

'Ah,' thought I, 'to be Captain William Dew,

R.N., and to have Mary to wife! What more could man desire?' and then I hastened towards her.

I saw by the turn of her eye that she was not over pleased to see me, for she made as if to walk away in the other direction, but I hastened towards her, and, seeing this, she waited for me.

'Are you frightened of me, or do you dislike me so much that you cannot even stop to speak to me, Mary?' I asked; and the figure of Will Bryant being in my mind made me speak somewhat wrathfully.

'Frightened, indeed! William Dew,' quoth she, and her black eyes flashed and sparkled angrily, 'a nice goose I should be to be frightened of a big boy like you.'

'Well, do you dislike me? And if I am but a big boy, you need not turn away because you happen to see me.'

'No, I don't dislike you. Why should I? But frightened, indeed!' and again she tossed her pretty little head, and drew tighter over her shoulders her scarlet cloak. 'Girls like me are not frightened at over-grown boys who spend their days following their father's plough, drink skim milk instead of good honest ale, and are regular ninnies.'

Now, to be called a ninny angered me, so I answered sharply that even if I was a ninny and followed my father's plough, it 'was better than smuggling and only pretending to work.'

Her white teeth shone from between her bright red lips in a scornful smile. 'Oh, you are very honest, I daresay; but if I were a man I wouldn't be such a coward as to be frightened to help land a cargo; at anyrate, I wouldn't stop all my life idling about a little village. I'd go and see the world like—'

'Like Lieutenant Fairfax, and come back with gold lace on my coat and make love to my sister's pretty maid.'

'No, I don't mean Mr Fairfax, and I am sure, if I did, it would be no business of yours. I was going to say like Will Bryant. So don't be so sharp, Mr Dew.'

This was the way we always talked when we had met lately, for I was very jealous; but I was no match for her at talking, and where, indeed, is the man who can match himself against a woman when the tongue is the weapon?

Of course, you will understand that in such a small place as Solcombe, everyone knew his neighbour's business, and the women folk of our village were ever ready to tell stories of one another; but 'tis the same everywhere, even in London. However, be that as it may, it was the regular talk of the village that young Mr Fairfax had been seen more than once making love to his sister's maid, and, though everyone supposed he was only idling, yet they all said that Mary took him seriously. Now, since those days, I have seen much of the world, and I do not think that one should always believe what women say of one another, especially where men's names are mentioned; but yet, at that time, I did suffer much mental tribulation as to whether Mary cared for the lieutenant as well as for Will Bryant—for of Will I did think she thought over much, and so, indeed, did others besides me, for the village folk said that Will had gained her heart, and that she only tolerated the lieutenant until the handsome young smuggler was ready to take her to his home.

When first Mary went to the Manor House, she had walked out with me more than once and given me some slight encouragement, but it only lasted a week or two, until Will Bryant came along, and then I saw my chance of gaining her heart was very doubtful. Pretty Miss Charlotte Fairfax, as I afterwards learned, had much to do with this, for she was always telling Mary what a fine, brave fellow this dare-devil Bryant was, and how it was a great thing for so young a man to have spitted two French privateersmen, one after another, as he had done, when they cut out the St Malo privateer. And, truth to say, it was no wonder the women admired him, for he was a big, strapping, handsome man, and, for his skill in a boat, exceeded by no man on the island.

But I was resolved that afternoon to have it out with Mary ; and so, presently, I went on, 'You must forgive me, Mary, but I can't bear to see you so friendly with a man whose father holds his head so high as old Squire Fairfax. You know that nothing can ever come of it—the old Squire would never allow it; and, Mary, dear, I can't bear to think of the unkind things people are sure to say if they see you together so often.'

'Well, I am sure, William Dew! How dare you preach to me in such a way, as if I were some silly child?'

'Mary, you know why I talk to you so. You know I love you dearly. If, when you gave me the cold shoulder for the sake of Will Bryant, I had thought he was worthy of you, I would have broken my heart before I would have spoken as I have done; but now that you speak as if you had thrown him over, as you threw me over for him, just because this gold-laced dandy has chosen to play with you, I must speak to you and speak for your good.'

She took a step forward and her eyes danced and sparkled with angry fire. 'William Dew, I will never speak to you as long as I live. I will never forgive you your impudence. Love me, indeed! Throw *you* over, indeed! Why, you silly, loutish goose, I never thought anything of you! You clod-hopping milksop, Will Bryant is worth a dozen of you! Go away like he has done and fight for your country, and try to come home and say that you, too, cut down two bigger men than yourself, as he has done, then you can have something to talk about; and if you don't come back with a gold-laced coat, you can, at anyrate, be thought a man. No girl with any spirit wants to talk to you now. So now, William Dew!' and she turned away with a truly fierce look upon her handsome face.

'One word, Mary. Would you think better of me if I volunteered and served a commission in the Service? Do you think I should have any chance when I came back?'

'As to chances, William Dew, I sha'n't say anything, because a girl don't know her mind for long, you know; but if even you had the courage to be a man and see the world, why, of course, everyone would think a great deal more of you.'

Then Mary turned her head and walked away, and left me to ponder on her words. Those words led to most of my misfortunes, for though, poor girl! I know now she only meant them to give me some sort of proper spirit, I took them as an encouragement of another kind, and forthwith resolved to try and be a man more to her liking. And, as I have said before, this led to my undoing.

CHAPTER III

I AM PERSUADED BY WILL BRYANT TO BECOME A MAN OF METTLE

I HAD now quite determined to enlist in the army or join the navy at the very first opportunity that presented itself, for the taunting words of Mary Broad had more than ever inflamed my mind in the matter. And so that I might become something of a man of the world, and rub off some of my rustic simplicity, I began to spend my evenings in the ale-houses near Solcombe, and study the loud talk and manners of those that frequented them.

One evening I was in a tavern at Ryde where I met Will Bryant. We fell a-talking, and in a while our talk came round to Mary Broad. Although I was so jealous of Bryant, he was such a big, good-natured, if idle and dissolute, fellow, that I could not feel very bitter towards him, and the pint or two of ale that he gave me to drink made my tongue somewhat loose. He understood how the land lay with me, and so far from resenting my admiration for his dark-eyed sweetheart, he seemed to feel a pity for me. Perhaps this

was because he regarded me but as an over-grown boy,
and so, after some little talk, we grew confidential,
and before we parted had become quite friendly.

It came about in this way. Will asked me if I had
seen Mary of late, 'For,' said he, with a good-natured
smile, 'she may have taken more kindly to you this
last week or two. I know that the wench has
deserted me for a long while.'

Then, all the while in a great fear lest I should
rouse his temper and feel the weight of his hand and
lead to mischief between him and the other, I told him
how Mary was carrying on with young Fairfax.

He leaned back and squared his great chest and
laughed heartily, and said, 'Oh, I know what the jade
is after. I don't mind that a bit. Young Fairfax
is as honest a gentleman as ever lived, and, look you,
William Dew,' and there came a curious look in his
eye, 'Mary is as good a girl as is in the world. 'Tis
only harmless fun they are having, though I know that
Master Fairfax really fancies himself in love with the
girl and would marry her to-morrow morning if he
could get to windward of the old man and talk him
into giving his consent. And that he is as likely to
get as I am to get the command of a seventy-four.
But Mary amuses herself with him, no doubt, by saying
she'll marry him when the Squire consents.'

'But don't you think—' I began, when he interrupted me.

'I don't think anything, William, my lad. The

girl, when she is tired of the game and when he's off
to sea again, will come back to me once more all right.
She's only backing and filling like this for a purpose.
I'm in no hurry, but, anyhow, it makes no difference.
When I'm ready I shall go and fetch her and marry
her, although some people would as lief she married
the devil, I believe.'

His easy, confident manner quite dashed my hopes
to the ground, for he was such a masterful fellow, and
I had seen before this what a great influence he had
over her that I felt he was right, and he could marry
the girl whenever he had a mind to it.

'But, William,' he went on, 'she's a good girl, and
when I do marry her, I'll give her a proper home, and
that I haven't got yet.   I like my freedom and so does
she, and we are in no hurry.'

'You take it coolly.   I wish I had your chance,
Will Bryant.   I'd willingly give up my freedom,' I
answered with some bitterness.

'Never mind, my lad.   Your turn will come some
day, and you'll find a maid who will make as good a
wife as Mary, only don't look so down in the mouth.
Why don't you take a trip to sea and have a look at
the world?   Why, lad, I don't believe that you have
ever been further than Portsmouth in your life.'

'You are right, Will.   I have seen nothing of life,
and I have been no further than to Portsmouth two
or three times and to Southampton once.   It is not
everyone that can get away in a king's ship and cut

out a French privateer as you have done. I would much like to get a run with some ship to the Indies, but I don't want to join the Merchant Service, and even if I did, there are few merchantmen about these parts, and no captain would care to ship me with so many sailors and fishermen to be had for their money.'

'Save us! Then why don't you get to learn something in that way? Come about with us a bit and learn to be handy in a boat. That would be better than following the plough tail and milking the cows all your life.'

By this time we had had another pint of ale and I was quiet pot valiant.

'I would he glad enough to do so,' I said, 'but I am very awkward in a boat, and would only be soundly rated for a fool if you had me in yours.'

'Look here, William, my lad, if you like you can help us without going into a boat. There is a little cargo to be landed not far from Solcombe Bay, and if you are a lad of mettle and care to give us a hand with it, you'll have a chance to pick up a trifle of pocket money, as well as a little experience, that will help to make a man of you.'

'Ah, Will,' I said, 'I know what you mean, but I don't want to mix myself up in any smuggling.'

'Why not?' he said earnestly. 'Your own father is one of the buyers of French brandy when it is landed. Why, even Squire Fairfax himself is not above buying the goods, so long as we are willing to take the risk of landing them.'

And so it was by clever speeches like this that Will Bryant led me to take part in my first and last smuggling adventure—that is, the last adventure in which I played the part of a smuggler, for it was not the last in which I played a part.   But of that hereafter.

CHAPTER IV

THE EVIL THAT BEFEL ME IN FOLLOWING
BAD ADVICE

So, a couple of nights later, according to a pot-valiant promise I had made him, I met Will Bryant about a mile from Solcombe, on a lonely spot near the water's edge. It was a very dark night, and though there was no wind, the breakers were showing white in the darkness as they dashed against the high cliffs on either side of the bay on the sandy beach of which we stood looking out to sea. We had come to look out for a lugger, and give her the signal that the coast was clear, and Will Bryant had for this purpose a horn lantern concealed under his oilskin coat.

In all conscience, I was very frightened, for I dreaded that, silent and dark as it was, some of the Preventive men might be about, and that I should be caught in this my first attempt to cheat His Majesty the King.

Presently my companion said, ' It must be nearly twelve o'clock, William. Stay you here while I go up on the cliff with the lantern. I can see the boat

from there when she comes near. Now, if you hear
the slightest sound or see a figure moving about, just
walk away quietly up the path and tell me. If anyone should speak to you, answer loudly, so that I can
hear, and then I should know that I must warn the
lads off. I shall be just above your head on the cliff,
lying down, and can hear anything.'

I answered in a whisper that I would do as he told
me, and then away he went up the path which led to
the top of the cliff, and left me standing, half-frightened
out of my wits and peering out into the darkness.

I must have stood like this but two or three minutes,
which seemed many hours, when I heard what sounded
like muffled footsteps as they trod upon the soft sand,
and the sound seemed to come from the path by which
Will Bryant had just ascended. I turned and moved
away a few paces, thinking that he had come back to
give me some more directions.

In an instant, and before I had time to realise what
had befallen me, I was seized by the arms, a cloak was
thrown over my head and my legs were knocked from
under me.

'Ram some of that oakum into his mouth and run
him through if he attempts to move,' said someone in
a whisper.

'Ay, ay, sir. He's quiet enough,' answered another
voice.

I knew what had happened, and I take pleasure to
remember that, frightened as I was, my first thought

was of Bryant and what he would think of me. Would he think I had betrayed him into the hands of the Preventive Service, for they were the Preventive Service, I knew?

But I had no cause to fear that. 'Drag him into the cave, and you, Ned Bolt, stand over him with your cutlass,' said the officer. 'You, Southgate, go up on the cliff and tell the others to bring the other bird down. Keep both of them gagged, and don't make a noise.'

And then, with cruel roughness, I was dragged into one of several small caves higher up the beach, and soon there came more footsteps and the sound of men struggling with an awkward burden, and Will Bryant was half-dragged, half-carried down the path, and then thrown into the cave beside me.

'Mr Belton, you go up on the cliff with that lantern, and as soon as you see the boat show the light three times in quick succession. When they run her up on the beach, if they hail, just answer " All well," and then come down and lend us a hand ; we shall want every man.'

Then I heard Mr Belton walk off, and thought fearfully of what was next likely to happen to me.

The officer give some more orders to his men, and then lit another lantern with his tinder box, and told them to take the cloaks off the prisoners and the gag from my mouth, so that he might have a look at us.

In the dim light I could see about a dozen Pre-

ventive Service men standing near with their hangers
drawn and pistols ready, and poor Will Bryant lay on
his back with a lump of oakum crammed into his
mouth for a gag, and his arms and legs lashed to keep
him from struggling.

As the light fell upon his pale and bleeding features,
he turned his eyes toward me with such a deadly look
of hatred in them that struck fear into my heart ; but
it lasted for but a moment when he saw that I too lay
bound and gagged, and then his glance softened, and I
knew he felt sorry he had led me into such a sore
predicament.

' Hullo ! ' said the officer, holding the lantern over
our faces, ' I know the pair of you, but I never
expected to catch you at this game, young Dew.   I
thought you were a regular psalm-singing, young
clodhopper.'

' It's the first time, lieutenant, I swear it's the first
time,' I said tremblingly, for I knew the officer, who
was a great, stout man, and quite friendly with my
father.

' Oh, of course.   But don't pipe your eye about it ;
you won't be thought any the more of for whining.
As for the other fellow, I know you, Will Bryant,
and by the Lord Harry you'll catch it this time !   I've
wanted you for a long while, my lad ; you're a regular
out-and-outer at the game.'

' You'll choke the man, sir,' I said beginning to
weep.   ' Take the gag out of his mouth.'

'No fear of that, my pious young friend; he'll be choked in another way. If I took the gag out, he'd sing out to the boat, which can't be far off now. I know him too well for that;' and with that he turned on his heel and went out of the cave.

Presently, he came back hurriedly and spoke hastily in an undertone to his men, and all save one followed him to the beach. The light in the cave had been put out before this and my eyes had grown accustomed to the darkness, and so I could see the bundle in the further end of the cave which I knew to be Will Bryant, as well as the face of the man who stood between him and myself with his drawn cutlass.

'Look here, youngster,' said he, 'take my advice and keep quiet or I'll run you through the first time you as much as wink your eye, and I'd be sorry to have to do it, for you're a young fellow, and I daresay you've got a mother.'

I began a reply, when he stopped me with a quick movement of his cutlass, as a hoarse voice from the cliff cried 'All well.'

Then I heard the grating of the boat's bottom as she was run up on the sandy beach, and the gruff whispers of the crew. The next moment the voice of the lieutenant rang sharply out on the still air,— 'Surrender, you are my prisoners!'

A yell of rage was the reply. Then came the clash of steel and several pistol shots, curses and oaths, and the sounds of a deadly struggle, and I lay and trembled and wondered how many were killed, and thought of what my father would say when he heard of it all on the morrow, and knew that his son was mixed up in such a terrible affair.

The fight did not last more than a few seconds, but to me, lying bound and helpless, it seemed hours. Then came footsteps and lights again, and a procession of the officers and their prisoners entered the cave.

There were only eight of them altogether, and they were far outnumbered by the Preventive Service men, who had wounded three or four of them slightly, while more than one of their captors was rubbing his head or tying up an arm or a leg, for the smugglers were not the men to be taken without giving hard knocks.

But the affray was nothing serious, and no one was hurt very much, although, to my unaccustomed eyes and ears, a most desperate and bloody battle had been fought.

The smugglers came into the cave cursing and swearing that they had been betrayed, and declaring that Will Bryant was the betrayer; but when they caught sight of him lying on the ground, bound hand and foot, they understood the wrong they did him.

Presently the officer ordered us to be ironed, and the gag was removed from poor Bryant's mouth. The first words he uttered were in my defence, and greatly endeared him to my mind at the time.

'You have caught us this time sure enough, Mr Lieutenant,' he said, 'but that boy has had nothing to do with it. I brought him with me for the first time, and he did not know what was going on.'

Then another of the smugglers broke in—a man who, when they had first been brought in, had had his face covered with his neck-cloth to staunch the blood flowing from a wound he had received in the fight. His name was Peter Collis, a near neighbour of ours at Solcombe, and a good-for-nothing fellow.

'What was Dew doing on the beach?' he said. 'He must have played the spy.' And several of the others cried out, 'Yes, yes, he's the informer.'

I was about to angrily protest my innocence of such base conduct when I caught Bryant's eye, and I saw it would advantage me to say nothing.

The lieutenant now ordered us to stow our jaw tackles and keep what we had to say for the magistrates, and then we were ordered to march. The guard fell in on either side of us with drawn cutlasses in their hands, and we were escorted to a guard-house near Newport, where we were lodged for the remainder of the night, and of all my companions, I think I suffered the greatest misery.

CHAPTER V

I WILL not relate in detail all the fear and grief that
fell upon me at finding myself a prisoner on such
a dreadful charge—as it was to my mind—of ob-
structing the King's Revenue Officers in their duty,
and the sorrow and shame of my father at finding
me in such a perilous situation.

On the morning after our capture, we were all
marched, handcuffed in pairs, into Newport, and
lodged in the market-place, to be examined by the
magistrate. Before entering the magistrate's room,
I was taken away separately by one of the Preventive Service men to another room, where my
father awaited me.

Meanwhile, the others were taken before the
magistrates — Squire Fairfax and our parson — the
latter a gentleman who was especially dreaded by
any smuggler that happened to be brought before
him, as he was a very harsh man, though he loved
the brandy that was smuggled well enough. Indeed,
so red was his nose, that the fisher-folk used to say

30

that it was as good as a riding-light on a dark night. Well, to make a long story short, the eight of them were committed for trial at the next Winchester Assizes.

As for the talk I had with my father, it was but little. His reproaches stung me so keenly that I could not, for my life, attempt to say much, and was glad when I was marched out again, though sadly ashamed to be had up like a common thief before the Squire and parson. Yet it was most lucky for me that it was Squire Fairfax, for father had seen him that morning, and, whatever it was that passed between them, it made things easier for me. Mr Sharpe, the great Newport attorney, had been engaged by my father to appear and say what there was to say on my behalf.

So he just told the magistrates the truth about the matter, and William Bryant was called for. Will came in, and in a very honest manner took all the blame upon himself for having led me astray, and the Squire gave him a severe talking to for his behaviour. Then Mr Fairfax, taking a pinch of snuff, turned to me and said,—

'I understand, my lad, that you have got mixed up with these law-breakers in a laudable desire to learn something besides following the plough—though that, indeed, is honest labour—in order that you might be of some service to your King and country. I am told that you are anxious to serve His Majesty—

God bless him!—and on my making that known to the King's officer, who laid you by the heels last night, I found that he is not anxious to press the charge against you, and so, the sooner you make up your mind, and volunteer for service, the better it will be for you. As for your fellow-prisoners, they were caught in very different circumstances, and it has been our duty to deal very differently with such villains.'

This was a surprise to me, and I muttered something, by way of thanks, in reply and left the room. My father followed me out, and in a broken voice said,—

'Well, William, you have your wish, and now you can take yourself off from the old place as soon as you have a mind to it.'

'What does he mean, and how has it all come about?' I asked.

And then father explained that he had told the Preventive Officer who had captured us, and Squire Fairfax as well, that I was mad to go soldiering or sailoring, and that this inclination had got me into this scrape.

Then young Lieutenant Fairfax, who was present at the time, remarked,—'Well, if the boy wants to go and make a man of himself, let him go, and I'll get him enlisted into my company and keep an eye upon him.'

'Well,' said the Preventive Officer, 'I won't stand

in his way, and won't press the charge, if Bryant
gives evidence confirming his story, and if he likes
to join the Marines, why, the Squire can acquit
him, and the Squire's son can enlist him, and there's
an end of it.'

A week later, and I had taken a sad farewell of
my father and his sister—my Aunt Dorothy, who
kept house for him—and was on my way to Portsmouth in a wherry to join the Marine depôt. Miserable enough I felt, I can tell you, as I stepped into
the boat in charge of a red-headed, but good-tempered,
corporal, who, all the way from Solcombe to Ryde,
where we embarked, tried to improve my spirits by
telling me stories of the practical jokes played by
his comrades on recruits, and warning me to take all
in good part, unless I was one who was free with
my hands.

My recollections of those days in barracks, and
all that befell me, are few; but, nothing that did
occur there had any influence on my after life. I
was not wanting in intelligence, and, indeed, though
'tis I who say it, I was something of a better sort
than the young men then enlisting. Thus I soon
got out of the awkward squad, and was reported as
drilled and fit for duty.

We were then quartered in Weevil Barracks,
and Lieutenant Fairfax had returned to duty at
the same time as I had joined my regiment, or
rather division. The Marines were in divisions, and,

c

of course, I belonged to the Portsmouth Division, and, by Mr Fairfax's influence, I was drafted into his company. He was a most honourable and generous man, and everything that he could do to encourage me to learn my duty he did, and did in such kindly fashion as made me deeply grateful to him, and anxious to do credit to his teaching.

While I lay in barracks learning to be a soldier, or rather a Marine—for there is all the difference between them, let me tell you—the smugglers were tried at Winchester Assizes, and were all of them, excepting poor Will Bryant, sentenced to five years in prison. But Will, because he received a bad character, was given a sentence of seven years. I thought a good deal of poor Mary Broad when I heard of this, for, said I to myself, the poor girl will be greatly upset at such woful news for her; but then I took comfort; and, if the truth was known, was rather glad at heart, as I thought, silly fool that I was, that this gave me a chance still to win her when I came back covered with glory from my first campaign and talking about foreign places and storming parties and the like.

But all these hopes were doomed to bitter disappointment, for the next news I heard of Mary proved how little I understood the great courage and affection that lay in her heart for Will Bryant.

One day Lieutenant Fairfax sent for me to his quarters, and I went there somewhat fluttered, for,

though this young Gentleman, by his kind and condescending manner to me, had so won my heart that
he was to my mind as great a man as a general,
he was yet so stern when he had to find fault that
I cannot truly say whether the men of his company
feared or loved him most.

'Come in, Dew,' said he, as I stood at the door
and saluted. 'Have you heard anything lately of
Mary Broad, my sister's maid? I think you were
a little sweet in that direction, eh, my lad?'

'No, sir,' I answered, with a great redness coming to my face; 'I think Mary is a good girl, and
I hope she is doing her duty in the Squire's service.'

'Well, I have some news that will surprise you.
Three or four days ago Bryant made a determined
attempt to escape from Winchester Gaol, and Mary,
who had previously disappeared from the Manor
House without leaving any message or clue as to
where she was going, has been caught in helping
the lusty smuggler out of gaol.'

This news staggered me, indeed, but I could scarcely
believe Mary would try such a dangerous thing as this,
and so, with all due respect, I ventured to tell the
lieutenant.

'All the same,' says he, "'tis true. She got into
the prison by bribing one of the warders and telling him that she was Bryant's sister, and she smuggled
in a rope and all sorts of gear, and just as the plot
was ripe and they were about to get away, the

whole thing was discovered, and the pair of them are now by the heels.'

'This is very bad, sir,' I managed to say. 'What will be done to her do you think, sir?'

'Hang 'em both, like as not, I am sorry to say.'

'Great heavens, sir! they'll surely not hang the woman. She is only a girl as yet, sir.'

'Hang 'em they will though, Dew, and although I am an officer in the King's Service, and you are only a private, and it's rank blasphemy to say so, I wish to the Lord they'd escaped and got clean away. Look you, Dew, Will Bryant is a devilish fine fellow, too good to be hanged, and the girl— well, the girl is too good for him. That will do, Dew, I have nothing more to say to you.'

There was a tear in my officer's eye as he said the last words, and turned away from me. As for me, I was too completely upset to feel anything but a dull sense that glory was of no use to me now, and so I went away to the barrack-room, and, lying down on my cot, turned my face to the wall and cried like the boy I was, heedless of the coarse jests and laughter of my comrades.

And for many a day after that the image of sweet Mary Broad was in my mind, until again I longed for nothing so much as active service, and for the time when I should meet that French or Spanish bullet whose billet would be my poor, wretched self.

CHAPTER VI

I MEET WITH A STARTLING ADVENTURE

THE Portsmouth Division of Marines, to which I was
attached, among its other duties was called upon to
furnish a guard to assist the Portsmouth Preventive
Service in guarding the long line of beach from Southsea Castle on the east to Gilkicker Point on the west,
and from these points the chain of sentries was continued right along the coast by men furnished from
the regiments stationed in this district. I was very
glad I was not stationed at Gilkicker, for 'twas at
this very place that Jack the Painter was hanged in
chains for setting fire to Portsmouth Dockyard, and
his remains still swung from the gibbet at the time
of which I write.

The ground covered by the Marines—who were
posted each one about a mile apart—covered a distance
of more than ten miles or so, and what with this, and
the many other guards required in a garrison town
like Portsmouth, it fell to my lot very often to spend
a solitary four hours on the look-out for smugglers—
doing 'sentry go' as they call it in the Service. It

was on an occasion like this that an event befell me which changed the whole course of my life.

It was on a night in December, 1786, that I was stationed as a sentry on the beach. My sentry-box was fixed about five hundred yards east of Southsea Castle, and the dark outline of its walls, though such a distance away, seemed to tower directly over my head. In those days sentries were only relieved every four hours on this particular duty, and visits from the officer of the guard were infrequent and irregular. My post—that is to say, the space of ground which I was supposed to cover—extended over a walk of about two hundred and fifty yards on each side of my sentry-box.

It was a pouring wet night, and the wind blew in fierce, bitter-cold gusts, and when I marched out to relieve my comrade at ten o'clock until two o'clock next morning, I had it in my mind to pass those weary hours in the shelter of my sentry-box. The post was not an important one, and the Preventive Service was supposed to do all the watching for the smugglers, while the Marines were only provided as a chain of sentries to assist the revenue officers when called upon. At least, that was the way in which we used to look at it, and mighty vexed we were at being employed upon such work.

When the sergeant marched me up to the post and the sentry going off had duly ported arms at the sentry going on duty, and we had mumbled over the order for the night, I was unpleasantly reminded of my duty, for, said the sergeant, turning to me, 'Look here, my fine fellow, see that you keep your eyes open to-night. We have heard that an attempt is likely to be made to run a cargo somewhere between here and Hayling Island. If you see a boat touch the beach, don't be in a hurry to challenge. Just let them get the cargo out of her, and keep you quiet. Then don't challenge, but fire, and call the attention of the guard.'

Our main guard was inside the gate at Southsea Castle, and I saw that if the smugglers did succeed in landing their cargo anywhere near my post, that, even if they got off themselves, the cargo would certainly be seized by the revenue officers. But then, I thought, it was scarcely likely that smugglers would choose a landing-place so near the Castle, where they knew our main guard was stationed. However, I made up my mind to keep wide-awake, and resolutely paced my five hundred yards, often fancying I heard, through the steadily-increasing howling of the wind and the stinging showers of rain any number of boats rowing in towards the shore, but never finding these alarms anything more than imagination.

At midnight I was visited by the sergeant making his rounds, and reported all well. The two hours that had already gone by seemed to me more than a whole night, and, after the sergeant was out of sight and hearing, I stood up for rest and shelter in

my box, and a moment or two later was straining
my ears and thinking, 'Surely that is the splash of
oars.'

Yes, this time I was right. It was high water,
and the waves now plashed up to within a few yards
of my feet. Between the gusts of wind and rain, I
could distinctly hear the sound of oars. I carefully
re-primed my musket and decided to remain inside
the box to keep the priming dry, and wait, as the
sergeant had directed me, until, if this was the
smuggling party, they should have had ample time
to get the cargo out.

In a few moments I heard the boat ground on the
beach, and fancied that I also heard voices in an
undertone; then the boat shoved off again—I could
hear that quite plainly. Presently, I heard the footsteps of one person on the shingle, and, before I had
time to bring my musket to the present, a voice
said,—

'Don't sing out, William, I have a message for
you.'

I knew the voice as that of a neighbour of ours
at Solcombe, and so for a moment my suspicions
were set at rest, but the next instant I remembered
that the man was a well-known smuggler, who only
by chance was not with the gang that was captured
when Will Bryant and his comrades were trapped,
and so I was on my guard again. 'What do you
want?' I asked.

'I bring you a message from Mary Broad and Will Bryant.'

'What of them, and how do you come by a message?' said I.

'Never mind how I came by the message, lad, but they send their love to you and bid you farewell, for 'tis likely you'll never see them again.'

'What! are they to be hanged, then? Lieutenant Fairfax told me his father was trying to get them reprieved.' This was true, for Mr Fairfax and the Parson and a number of the great people on the Isle of Wight had been doing all they could to save the poor creatures from death.

'Oh, they're not going to be hanged, but they will be sent to Botany Bay, and so, my lad, they have sent their farewell to you.'

'Dear, dear me, this is dreadful. Why, that is worse than death. I've heard it said that it is more than likely that those who are sent there will be eaten by the cannibals if they are not starved to death. But,' and again I began to remember that he who spoke was a great rogue, 'why do you come here at this time of night to tell me this? Don't you know that I might have shot you, or turned out the guard, because, look you, I know you must be in company with the smugglers that we are expecting?'

The man laughed. 'I know that,' said he, 'and the boat I came in was the lugger's, sure enough, but there will be no cargo landed to-night.'

'Ah,' said I, with foolish vanity, 'we are too clever for you, are we?'

'Yes, we knew you were all on the alert, and so, what with the bad weather and the danger from your fellows, the lugger has put to sea again. I wanted to come to Portsmouth, and so they landed me before they ran out.'

'What, after the narrow escape that they had when Will Bryant tried to run his cargo, are you still risking your neck in this business?'

'No, that's just it. I ran over to the coast of France and back in the vessel, because I had promised to go this trip, but they have let me off now, and I wash my hands of the whole lot.'

'Well, I'm right glad to hear it, and I hope you'll take to something honest now.'

'Yes, that I will, William, my lad; but I won't join the Marines and have to spend four hours on a night like this on the beach.'

Presently I asked him how it was he knew where to find me.

'Oh,' says he, 'one of the hands on the lugger —a spy of ours—said he had heard some of the Marines say in the ale house that young Dew had the first post west of the Castle, and I thought I would get the boat to land me somewhere about here so that I could give you poor Mary's message. Well, good-bye, William. But, here, I forgot. I've got something here to keep out the cold and wet.

Take a pull ; ' and with this he handed me a flask of spirits.

I took a drink, and I have some remembrance of repeating the act more than once, but I recollect nothing else that passed that night, and what happened afterwards is best told in the words of the officer of the guard. This is from his report :—

'At two o'clock on the morning of December the twenty-first, I went with Sergeant Brookes and two privates to inspect the guard and relieve Private Dew, at number one post, west side of Southsea Castle. The night was very dark, and half a gale of wind was blowing, with every now and then very fierce squalls of rain. We could not find the sentry, and the sentry-box had disappeared. There were many signs that a landing had been made and a cargo run on the beach at this post. Private Dew had been visited at mid-night by the sergeant and all was then well. When daylight came it showed, as was suspected, that the smugglers were the cause of his disappearance. There were marks of men and horses about the place, and the shingle showed that more than one boat had been run up on the beach, and heavy weights, such as casks, had been rolled over it. For the rest of the night I doubled the guard and continued the search for Private Dew, but up to the present have found no traces of him.'

This report was handed to the commanding officer

early on the morning of the twenty-first. A few hours later a dragoon orderly galloped into barracks and handed to the colonel the following message :—

'At daylight this morning the sentry at number eighteen post, near Gilkicker Point, saw an object which looked like a sentry-box, on a small sand shoal partially covered with water near the Mother Bank. The officer of the guard sent off a boat with a sergeant and two privates to inquire into the matter, and in a short time the boat returned and brought back Private Dew of the Marines and his sentry-box. The man was in a half-dazed condition and is either recovering from drink or from the effects of some drug. He is unable to give any coherent account of how he got on the Mother Bank. He is now a prisoner at the fort, under charge of the surgeon.'

This was signed by the officer in charge of the guard at Blockhouse Fort.

Well, to make a long story short, the smuggler rogue had drugged me, and, until the surgeon brought me to myself at Blockhouse Fort, I was ignorant of all that had happened.

When I did come to, I was, in pursuance of the Colonel's orders, marched off under an escort to the Clink, as we soldiers called the military prison, and there I remained for two days suffering much shame in spirit, and an object of curiosity to the soldiers who were my fellow-prisoners and to the men who formed the prison guard. The fear of being flogged, and perhaps shot, for deserting my post, and the open gibes of my comrades, made those days live long in my memory, and the lesson they gave me, more than anything else, made strict attention to duty, utterly regardless of private friends, my very first consideration. And though no man ever escaped from such a neglect of duty as lightly as I did, the fright I had in those two days lasted me all my life in the Service.

After some days, the colonel in command of the Portsmouth Division of Marines sent for me, and I was escorted to Weevil Barracks to be, as I thought, tried by court-martial and flogged for deserting my post.

The colonel was seated at a table with three or four other officers, including the captain of my company, and, to my great joy and comfort, for I knew I had a friend in him, Lieutenant Fairfax.

I saluted and stood to attention, and the lieutenant smiled encouragingly at me.

'Now, my lad,' said the colonel, 'don't be frightened. There's no need to let your hair stand up like priming wires. Tell us the whole truth about this affair, and I will do what I can for you. Your captain says you have the making of a good soldier in you, and you have a friend here in Lieutenant Fairfax. I don't believe in flogging men who get

into trouble through inexperience, and if you can
but show me some reason for leaving your post and
taking a cruise in your sentry-box and mounting a
new guard at the Mother Bank, miles from your post,
by George' (and I saw the old fellow and the rest of
them trying hard to avoid laughing), 'why, I'll forgive you.'

Then, with a shamed-faced air, I have no doubt, I
told them about the smuggler and my former acquaintance with his sort, and asked Lieutenant Fairfax to
confirm my story that far, which he did, adding that
I was a mere inexperienced boy, that the scoundrels
had taken advantage of me, and then, like the kind-
hearted Gentleman he ever was, he added that he had
no doubt that this second lesson in the wickedness of
the smugglers would last me all my life.

'That it will, gentlemen,' said I, my heart taking a
great leap of courage at his good words, 'for if ever I
drop across the rascal again it will go hard with
him.'

When they had questioned me fully as to the
manner of my being drugged, the colonel turned to
his fellow-officers.

'Well, gentlemen, it is plain that the lad was
drugged by this man, and that, when the drug had
taken effect upon his silly head, the smugglers ran
their cargo, and then, curse their impudence, out of
bravado carried away the sentry and his box in the
lugger and left him on the Mother Bank on their

way back to their haunts at the back of the Isle of
Wight, or the coast of France.'

'No doubt, sir, that is what did take place,' said
Lieutenant Fairfax; 'and he had a narrow escape of
being drowned, for the tide often covers the spot by
several feet where they found him.'

'Now, my lad,' continued the colonel, 'I will give
you a chance. This affair has got about. All the
garrison has heard of it, from the General downwards,
and everyone is looking to see you get a flogging, and
I'm not sure that you don't deserve it for being such a
fool. However, as I said, I'll give you a chance. We
want volunteers for the fleet now preparing to sail
for Botany Bay. Lieutenant Fairfax is one of the
officers of the Marine force going there, and he has
asked me to let you volunteer as one of the Marine
convict guard. I can't get our men to come
forward very readily, the frightened rascals, and
volunteer for the Service.' (And then aside to my
captain, 'And I'm hanged if I don't think they are
right.') But some of you must go. Now, if you will
volunteer cheerfully, I'll contrive to hush up this piece
of foolishness on your part. Come, what is it to be?'

Shame and grief at this ending to my ambition to
become a soldier brought the tears to my eyes, and I
hesitated for a moment and then thought of the
greater shame of the cat and triangles, and I
answered,—

'Thank you, sir, for giving me the chance. I

am sure your honour won't think the worse of me
being disappointed at losing the chance to serve in
foreign wars. I didn't join the Service to become a
gaoler.'

'Tut, tut, my lad, never mind, you'll get your
chance some day. Meanwhile, do your duty on this
service, and don't let these gaol birds make a fool of
you as easily as the smugglers did. Release the
prisoner, and, Captain Weston, enter Dew's name on
the list of volunteers for the *Sirius.*'

CHAPTER VII

I AM AGAIN FOOLED BY THE SMUGGLERS

THE First Fleet, as the Expedition was soon after named, was now all assembled and lying off the Mother Bank, that shoal in the Solent on which I had been left by the smugglers when they played their scurvy trick.

The Fleet was expected to sail in a day after the day I had joined the *Sirius*, and little leisure was given me to say farewell to my father and the Solcombe folks; so I wrote a few lines wishing them good-bye, sent the letter over to the island by a Ryde fisherman and settled down to my duty.

When I was rated on board the *Sirius* on Monday the sixth of May, 1787—a date ever to be remembered by me—I was astonished at the great state of confusion upon her decks. Everything was so vastly different to all I had heard of the neatness and cleanness of a ship of war, but all this arose from the nature of the undertaking in which the ship was engaged. All sorts of strange stores had to be carried, and so many things to be provided, that it was no

D

wonder that those in authority on board the Fleet were at their wits' ends where to stow them.

Each transport, in addition to the ordinary stores, carried a great quantity of implements of agriculture, seeds and such like things, and some extra clothing, such as woollen stockings, shoes, hats and slops of various kinds. The Marines, besides getting a little extra pay, were also provided with some light clothing suited to the climate of Botany Bay, where we expected to remain about five years, and these things had by some means been sadly mixed with the prisoners' clothing, through some of these articles having been put on board the *Sirius* in place of the powder and shot she would have carried in a more honourable service. So, owing to all the hurry and confusion, my awkwardness on first doing duty on shipboard was not noticed, and I escaped the curses and jibes that the Marines generally come in for from the sailors when the red-coats go to sea for the first time.

The principal officers on the *Sirius* were Captain Phillip, Captain Hunter (the second in command), Major Ross (our commanding officer) and Lieutenant King. Besides these, there were the surgeon and Judge-Advocate Collins, and some other Gentlemen whose names now I cannot recall.

Even amid all this turmoil I thought very often of Mary Broad and Will Bryant, and long before had asked Lieutenant Fairfax in a respectful manner if he knew aught of them.

'Yes, Dew,' he replied, 'and I'll willingly tell you all I know about them. Bryant is embarked on one of the transports—which one I do not know—and my father has interceded so far on his behalf as to have secured a promise from the authorities that he shall be a free man shortly after our arrival, but he will not be allowed to return till his sentence has expired.'

'That was very good of the Squire, sir,' I said; 'but what of the misguided young woman?'

'By George! Dew, Mary may be a misguided young woman, but she has a devilish fine spirit all the same;' and with that he told me that the Squire had sent the Parson to see her at Winchester Jail, so that he might get her in a humble frame of mind, and then he was to endeavour to procure her a pardon. 'And what think you, she said?' asked the lieutenant.

'I suppose, sir, she expressed her sorrow for her folly, and thanked the Squire.'

'Nothing of the sort. She begged the Parson to do his best to get her sent away with Bryant, or at all events, with the female prisoners going out with us. So the Squire said as that appeared to be all she was good for—my sister and myself couldn't see any reason why she shouldn't have her own way—he would do his best to get her exiled. That will do, Dew, I have nothing further to say to you.'

That was the way the lieutenant always finished up these little chats of ours, as a reminder, I suppose, of the difference in our rank, which was very proper

on his part, for 'twas a great piece of condescension for
a commissioned officer to talk of old times like this
with one of his men.

This was all the news I could get of the unfortunate smuggler or of Mary, and, although I did make
inquiries of the guards on the other ships, the prisoners
were always kept in such a way that, right up to the
day of our sailing, I never learned whether or not anyone I knew was on board of the transports. All I
heard was that most of the prisoners were selected
from the county jails on account of their supposed
knowledge of agriculture, but the women were nearly
all the most depraved characters taken from Newgate ;
and, somehow, I did not think Mary would be among
them.

And now I come to my last adventure with the
smugglers, and when I look back at it now, I think it
quite a wonder that I was not transported for my silly
way of being taken in by these people, who seemed to
mark my ignorance and pursued me with their tricks
in quite a marvellous manner.

The lieutenant, full of consideration for my inexperience, and, perhaps, because he liked to have me about
him, called me to him one day, and said,—

' I have sent for you, Dew, to make you an offer
which you are at liberty to refuse or accept as you
please. By the rules of the Service I am entitled to
one of the men in my company to attend upon me.
You can act in that capacity if you like. Of course,

Dew, I can understand that a young farmer, as you were, may have some scruples about acting as a servant, but all the privates are of equal rank here, and this duty may relieve you, perhaps, from still more menial work at sea, for, I can tell you, the Marines are thought precious little of by these coarse, dirty sailors.'

I thanked the young Gentleman heartily for his offer, and gladly enough accepted it, and, though our positions are very different now, I say with truth that I am proud of having served so good and honourable a master.

A day or two after this, the first cutter was sent ashore to the Point at Portsmouth to bring off some stores for the ship, and, in addition to the boat's crew, Lieutenant Fairfax came with us to perform some duty on shore, and another Marine and myself were sent with the boat to help in embarking the stores.

While I was helping to put some of the stores into the boat, an old waterman rowed his wherry into the landing-place, and calling to me asked if our party belonged to the *Sirius*.

'Yes,' said I.

'Oh, that's all right, then,' said he. 'What officer is with you?'

'My lieutenant, Mr Fairfax,' said I; 'he will be back to the boat directly.'

'Ah! that's the very thing. Well, you'd better bear a hand and get on with the job so as to be ready to shove off when he comes back.'

'What job?'

'Why, you see this cask of ale?' pointing to a big cask marked thus, XXX. 'Well, he wants this changed. They have sent off the wrong ale, and it goes agin his stummick, I suppose, and I've just brought it from your ship. They told me aboard that I'd find him at the Point, and some of his boat's crew would lend me a hand.'

'What are we to do?'

'Help me roll it up the street to the "Star and Garter," that's where he got it from.'

And so, after four of us had got the cask out of the boat, I helped the man roll it up the High Street, and very quick we were about it, for the old fellow said that Mr Fairfax would kick up a great row if the job wasn't done quickly, as the ale should have been changed long before.

As soon as we had rolled the cask up the roadway from the Point to the street, a Preventive Service officer stepped up, took a look at it and turned enquiringly to me.

'Officers' stores,' said the waterman, without waiting to be questioned.

'Cask of ale returned by my officer, Lieutenant Fairfax,' I added.

'All right, my lads,' said the officer, and he made a chalk mark on the cask and away we rolled it.

The 'Star and Garter' was not far up the street, but

it was, owing to a turn in the road, out of sight of the
Point. When he reached the door of the inn, the old
waterman turned to me, and said, 'Thank you, my
lad, here's the price of a glass of ale for you, and some
day I'll do you a good turn—by George! I'll do you
one now. Take my advice, and when you get to
Botany Bay keep your weather eye lifting a bit more
than you are doing now.'

'What do you mean?' said I, angrily.

'I'll tell you,' he answered, with a rude grin, 'but
take my advice and don't tell anyone else. This cask
is not going to the "Star and Garter." 'Cause why?
'Cause it's going to my place. It's not ale, it's best
French brandy.'

'What do you mean?' I again asked. 'Does not
the cask belong to my lieutenant?'

'Certainly not, my young lobster. It's smuggled
brandy.'

'You infernal old rascal! I see you have taken
advantage of my uniform to land your cask of brandy,
and this time I shall be ruined. Never mind, whatever happens, I'll go at once and inform the Preventive
Officer.'

'Oh, no, you won't. No one will know if you
keep your mouth shut, but if you inform the officer
you will only get yourself into trouble.'

'Ah, here comes Lieutenant Fairfax, and he has
seen me with you. I'll tell him and see what he has
to say about the matter.'

'Yes, tell him, Joey; he'll only laugh at you. Hang me! I'll tell him myself.'

Mr Fairfax, seeing me talking to the man and so far away from the boat, stepped over to us, and the old waterman, touching his hat, said,—

'Beg pardon, yer honour, but I borrowed the loan of one of your Joeys, who seems pretty green;' and then to my shame, he unblushingly told him the whole story.

Mr Fairfax laughed heartily, and said, 'You old rascal, you deserve the brandy for your smartness. We'll say no more about it,' and, turning to me, he added, 'but I really think, Dew, that this should be the last of your smuggling adventures. It is a good job for the pair of you that we sail for the other side of the world in a few days, or you would both hear more about it. However, the best thing we can do is to forget it now, and remember, my lad, that this sort of thing won't do in the future. We shall have you letting some of our prisoners escape if you don't use your wits more than you have been doing lately. That will do, Dew. Get into the boat.'

CHAPTER VIII

It is proper, before going further with the Narrative of my life, that I should give you some account of the preparations that were going on for the despatch of the Expedition. It is not my desire to attempt a history of the Settlement in New Holland, or, as it is now called, New South Wales; you must go to the books for that. Such things as I have set down are just facts taken from my notes in the rough diary of my life, set down without any scholarly skill, but yet truthfully.

The fleet was made up of two war vessels and nine transports. The *Sirius* of twenty guns, six hundred and twelve tons, and one hundred and sixty men, flew the broad pennant of Commodore Arthur Phillip, who commanded the Expedition, and who was to be the first governor of the settlement. The *Sirius* was supposed to be a frigate, but she was never built for war, and the sailors did not speak well of her sea-going qualities, so that we Marines, in addition to the other miseries we suffered,

57

did not feel at all safe on board of her. She was
built on the Thames to trade to the East, but, on
loading her with her first cargo, she took fire and
was nearly destroyed. This was in the year 1781,
and the Government, wanting a store-ship, purchased
her, and she made a voyage to the American colonies
and back under the name of the *Berwick*. Then
she made another voyage to the West Indies, and
was then laid up in ordinary at Deptford Yard, until
the time came when the Government planned this
Expedition, and the shipwrights overhauled her and
fitted her out to fly the flag of Commodore Phillip.

The *Supply* was a little, armed tender of one
hundred and seventy tons and eight guns and fifty
men. Lieutenant Ball had command of her. The
rest of the ships were transports taken up for the
Service, and, although I took pains to find out many
details concerning the Expedition, I will not here set
them down lest I make this Narrative too tedious;
so of these transports I need but say that their
complement, not counting their seamen, was as
follows :—*Alexander*, one hundred and ninety-four
male convicts, thirty-five Marines ; *Lady Penrhyn*,
one hundred and one female convicts and some
Marine officers ; *Charlotte*, one hundred and six male
and female convicts, forty-two Marines ; *Friendship*,
ninety-seven convicts, forty Marines ; *Prince of Wales*,
two male and forty-seven female convicts, twenty-
nine Marines ; *Scarboro*, two hundred and five male

convicts, forty-four Marines. And then there were three store-ships — the *Fishburn*, *Golden Grove* and *Borrodale*. On the two war vessels there were no convicts—or prisoners, as it became the custom of the Service to call them—but there were several officers and civil officials appointed to serve on the staff of Captain Phillip when he should assume the governorship of the Settlement. On the *Sirius* there was a Marine guard of a sergeant, six privates and two drummers, and I was mightily pleased that I was not chosen to do duty on one of the transports. Altogether the number of people on board the various ships who were to form the settlement was about one thousand and twenty. I must not forget to say that among the officials were a chaplain (who brought with him his wife) and a surgeon and five assistant surgeons ; and terrible botchers were some of these last.

The transports varied in tonnage from three hundred and fifty tons to two hundred and seventy-five tons, and every one of them was crowded in a very dreadful manner, and, long before the fleet got under weigh, sickness broke out both among the prisoners and the crews and the Marines ; indeed, on the *Alexander*, some of the Marines died of a malignant sickness, caused by the foulness of the air between decks.

At this time the trial of Lord George Gordon, the impeachment of Warren Hastings and other great State affairs, so disturbed the minds of the Govern-

ment that they gave but little thought to the fearful condition of the wretched creatures who were
going to Botany Bay, although the case of the wife
and children of a Marine, who nearly perished of
starvation on board one of the transports, was made
public in some way.

But bad as things were, even for us Marines, they
would have been worse but for Major Ross, who
fought hard to get us proper food and berthing space,
and, finally, we got pretty well served as far as food
went, for the rations allowed to each man for one
week were as follows :—Seven pounds of bread (hard
ship biscuit), four pounds of beef, two pounds of
pork, two pints of pease, three pints of oatmeal,
three and a half pints of rum, six ounces of butter—
and terribly rank-smelling stuff it was—three-quarters
of a pound of cheese and half a pint of vinegar.
These were to be added to in case we touched at
any port where fresh provisions could be had, and
we were in this matter fed the same as seamen in
the King's ships. As for the prisoners, they were
rationed in much the same way, but, in case of bad
conduct or breaches of discipline, they were made
to suffer by having their rations cut down. But
many of these articles that I have mentioned were
not fit for human food ; indeed, I heard Major Ross
tell Captain Hunter that the butter, cheese and beet
were such that a well-conditioned hog would have
turned away from them with a sickness of stomach.

As to the manner in which the transports were
fitted up I will speak briefly. Abaft the mainmast
in each ship was built a strong bulkhead of thick
wood, and in the forward side—that is, the convicts'
side—this bulkhead was studded with stout, sharp
spikes, and loopholed so that the guard could fire
upon the prisoners in case of mutiny. The hatches
were battened across with thick bars, bolted and locked
to the coamings, and railed round with strong, high,
wooden stanchions, so as to guard against a sudden rush
from below. Of course, sentries were placed over
each hatchway and at different parts of the ship,
and the main-guard was always kept under arms on
the quarter-deck with loaded muskets. On the upper
deck, abaft the mainmast, was built a barricade of
stout planks studded along the top with sharp, iron
prongs, and in the space between this and the head
of the ship the convicts were exercised.

Truly, it was a dreadful sight to see them caged
up like this, and yet more dreadful to hear their foul
and blasphemous talk among themselves, and their
horrible jests about their sad condition — for most
of them were utterly steeped in wickedness. Many
of them, before being sent on board the fleet, had
been kept in hulks at Portsmouth, Plymouth and
the Thames, and some of the transports had embarked their loads of human misery at these places,
and sailed round to the rendezvous before I joined
the *Sirius*. The *Alexander* and *Lady Penrhyn* had

embarked their prisoners in the Thames, and she had convoyed them round to Spithead early in the year, and they lay close to where the *Royal George* had sunk three or four years before this time, her masts being still to be seen sticking up out of the water. Long before I joined, the *Scarboro* and *Prince of Wales* and the three store-ships were already lying at anchor off the Mother Bank, and, indeed, were there on the very night when I cut such a pretty figure on the shoal.

On the sixth of March all the prisoners were embarked, and the *Charlotte* and *Friendship* sailed round from Plymouth and dropped anchor with the rest of the fleet; yet it was not until the second week in May that our good and esteemed Commodore, Captain Phillip, arrived from London, and great was the anger he showed at the deplorable state of confusion and misery that existed on board the ships of the Expedition, which seemed fated to be continually delayed from this or that cause, so that not only Captain Phillip but everyone else on board was sick and wearied at heart and anxious to get away. The Commodore spent most of his time running backwards and forwards to the dockyard people, trying to get them to make the rascally contractors serve us honestly, and as for Captain Hunter and his officers, they were too busy to trouble much about the Marines, and so we spent most of our time in looking after the officers' luggage and such work.

At last we did draw near the day of our sailing. The ships' companies of the *Sirius* and *Supply* were paid a two months' advance, and, forthwith, many of them got drunk with the bad grog brought off by the bumboat women of Portsmouth and Gosport, and assailed many of my comrades with extraordinary foul words and blows, and this increased the vexations and difficulties of our getting under weigh. Then, even when the warships were ready, the transports were not. The seamen of the *Fishburn* then refused duty, owing to a quarrel with the master, and, almost at the same time, those of the *Alexander* had to be replaced by a crew from the *Hyæna* frigate, because the poor fellows in the transport had not received their wages from the contractors, and refused to sail.

A strong westerly wind at the last moment still further delayed the fleet, and so it was not until Sunday, the twelfth of May, that the voyage fairly began, and we were not clear of the Needles for twenty-four hours later, and I think that every man must have said, 'Thank God!' For all the many delays and trials had had one good effect — there were no sorrowful farewells to add to the misery of the main body of our unhappy voyagers. They had all been made long before. The sorrowing wives, mothers and sweethearts of freemen and bondmen alike, had long since dried their tears and gone back to their homes, where, for many a weary day, they waited to hear tidings of the exiles. In those days, you must remember, there were no railway trains nor fast steamships, and folks travelled but little, so most of the good-byes were said far away from the rendezvous. In the case of the convicts, of whom the greater number came from jails and hulks all over the kingdom, there were few free people who came to say good-bye to them at Portsmouth; but the wives of some of the officers and men of the Marines came there to see us off, but the great delay had exhausted the moneys of the poorer sort, and they had long before returned to their homes. As for me, my father wrote and wished me well, and hoped that I would do my duty, but he came not near me, and I felt that he had not forgiven me the disgrace I had brought upon him.

I heard afterwards, that the prisoners on the transports — and the women in particular — grew quite cheerful at the sounds of the seamen heaving up the anchors, and many of them, in their horrible prisons below, joined in the sailors' choruses as the men tramped round the capstan. None would have thought that the poor creatures were banished from their native land and for ever, but the English prisons and the hulks were fearful places in those days, and 'twas no wonder that while I, and freemen such as I, saw the white cliffs of the Isle of Wight sink gradually out of sight with sorrowful feelings, that these poor creatures thought only of the horrors they were leaving behind them.

Our Commodore had already given proof that he was a humane and good man — a man not to be trifled with in his duty, but anxious to be just and do what was right in the sight of God, and a man of this quality was just the sort of governor to earn the respect of the class he had to deal with. I remember Lieutenant Fairfax telling me that one day when the Commodore had boarded the *Prince of Wales*, and had seen the horrible condition of the women's quarters that his eyes had filled with tears of pity, and he had used some pretty strong words about the cruelty of the thing, and said it was worse than a slaver's hold in the Middle Passage.

As soon as the fleet was fairly under weigh, the Commodore directed the master of the *Sirius* to heave-to, and then signalled for the commanding officer on the *Supply*, with a Marine officer and assistant surgeon from each transport, to come on board our ship. Each one, as he came on board, went on to the poop, saluted the Commodore and waited with some curiosity as to what he desired of them.

I was stationed as sentry over the stern life-buoy, and heard all that was said when they were assembled. The Commodore, looking intently into their faces and speaking very earnestly and clearly, said,—

'Gentlemen, I have sent for you all, now that we

F

are fairly under weigh, to repeat the instructions I have before given to you individually. I know you are all good officers, and anxious to do your duty to His Majesty; no doubt on that score troubles me. But I beseech you, Gentlemen, to endeavour to do all in your power to treat your prisoners with every consideration that will be likely to encourage them to good behaviour. We know that they belong to the lowest and most depraved class of our countrymen, but this Expedition has not been formed to punish them on that account, but rather to give them an opportunity to redeem themselves in a new world. So, with a view to preparing them for their new life, I should like you to avoid as much as possible treating them in the style they have hitherto experienced in the jails and hulks in England.'

He paused for a moment, and then, in somewhat quicker and more decisive tones, resumed,—

'But, Gentlemen, at the same time I should like you to bear well in mind that insubordination must be punished with even greater severity than it would be on land. Therefore, let your prisoners understand that any attempt at mutiny or escape will be punished with instant death. Of course, irons must never be placed upon the women, no matter how bad or dangerous their conduct may be, and as soon as we are clear of the Channel remove the irons from the men, so that they may be able to keep their bodies clean, and rest like human beings at night. This,

Gentlemen, with your written orders and my previous injunctions, is all I have to say to you to guide you in your responsibilities until we arrive.'

He ceased, and the officers, respectfully bowing, were about to leave the quarter-deck when Captain Phillip raised his hand, and said in his gentlest tones, 'Stay, Gentlemen ; one word more. While we were in Portsmouth I heard one of you—and I beg of him to take no offence at what I now say—remark that we were employed upon a service that would bring us neither credit nor distinction, but rather contempt. I implore you, Gentlemen, not to entertain such an unworthy opinion, for what can be more honourable than devoting ourselves to ameliorating and raising to a higher level in society these unfortunate outcasts and criminals ? May God assist us to fulfil, not only our duty to His Majesty the King, but our duty to the Amighty Himself.'

Then the Commodore shook hands with every one of them, a cheerful smile lightening up his face the while, and the officers returned to their ships, the yards were swung round, the sails filled and we stood away on our course down Channel.

CHAPTER IX

CONCERNING SOME INCIDENTS THAT HAPPENED
ON THE VOYAGE

THE *Hyæna* frigate accompanied us until we were clear of the Channel, and then on May the twentieth she hove-to for Captain Phillip's last despatches, and left us to return to Plymouth.

Ere she had signalled 'good-bye' to us, the first trouble with the convicts began. Mr John Marshall, the master of the *Scarboro*, came on board the *Sirius* and reported that there was a plot among his prisoners to seize the ship.

Lieutenant Fairfax and the whole of the Marines in the *Sirius* were at once sent away to the *Scarboro* to bring back the ringleaders. When we got on board we were drawn up on either side of the main hatchway, and then the surgeon, Mr Fairfax and Mr Marshall went down the ladder to the 'tween decks and spoke through the barricade to the prisoners, who had all gathered together behind the heavy wooden grating, peering anxiously through the bars and wondering what was to happen to them.

' Now, my lads,' said the surgeon, ' we know all about
it, and know the ringleaders. We want those men.
As for the rest of you, your treatment depends upon
your future conduct. Stand back from the grating
all of you.'

They all fell back several paces.

' Now, men,' continued the surgeon, ' we have
plenty of Marines here ready to fire into you if you
attempt any tricks, so remain where you are except
numbers four hundred and seventeen and two hundred
and nineteen. Phillip Farrell and Thomas Griffith,
advance to the grating.'

They stepped out. The Marine sentry, at a sign
from the surgeon, unlocked the gate, the surgeon
beckoned them to come out and the instant they
did so the gate was locked again.

' You men will hear no more of this if you mind
your bearings,' said the doctor, as he turned to ascend
the ladder. ' As for these two fellows, I don't think
they will try any more games of this kind.'

We brought numbers four hundred and seventeen
and two hundred and nineteen to the *Sirius*, and they
had to face the Commodore who, to my mind, gave
them a very mild reproof considering the serious
nature of their offence, cautioned them about their
future behaviour and promised to hang them at the
yard-arm if he heard more of them. Then he
ordered them to receive six dozen lashes each, and
accordingly they were seized to a grating and flogged

by two of our drummers, and afterwards placed on
board the *Prince of Wales*. The spectacle was a
very dreadful one, and I shall never forget the feeling
of horror that I experienced in witnessing their
punishment. There were no signs of mutiny after
this from the day of sailing to the time we cast
anchor in Botany Bay, and the demeanour of all
was, on the whole, humble and regular, save on one
occasion, of which I shall speak later on.

By this time I was acting as a ward-room servant,
in addition to my duties in attending upon my
lieutenant. In this situation I heard, while waiting
upon the officers, many things that otherwise would
never have come to my ears. My comrades were
all very ignorant rustics recruited from Hampshire
and Sussex, and of the Marine privates on the *Sirius*,
I was the only one who could read and write, and
perhaps, for that reason was made more of by my
superiors. All the officers on the ship were keeping
some kind of a journal of the Expedition, it being such
an extraordinary undertaking that none on board
the *Sirius* had ever embarked in the like before. My
comrades being such poor and unsuitable companions
even for a man of my humble attainments, the example
of my superiors, and the many things I heard at the
officers' mess, gave me the idea that I might take
advantage of my learning and likewise keep a Diary,
and so this record of my life was at this time begun.

Fortunately, I was no lover of grog, and so I used

to change my allowance with the sergeant for all
the spare paper he had, and my lieutenant furnished
me with quills and ink, so that, I was soon set up
with all that was necessary. This incident of chang-
ing my grog allowance reminds me that, strange to
relate, the poor prisoners suffered more from the want
of strong drink and tobacco than from any other hardships, for I heard Surgeon White tell the Commodore
that they pleaded very piteously for these things.

The fleet arrived at Teneriffe on the third of June,
and great joy did it give the Marines and ships'
companies, for everyone was allowed a pint of wine
a day and fresh provisions all the time we lay in the
port of Santa Cruz. The convicts, too, were well
treated, for the Commodore ordered each of them
to be given a pound of beef and a like quantity of
soft bread.

During our stay at Santa Cruz, more than one
incident happened, the which I set down with great
care in my diary. The first matter I overheard was
that the officers were not a little troubled over us
Marines having been sent away with a very scant
supply of musket balls, and there were no armourers'
tools in the whole fleet. This was kept as secret
as possible, but the guards in the different ships got
to hear of it, and it made them mighty careful to be
on the alert to check any attempt at mutiny. Both
Captain Phillip and Captain Hunter were greatly
vexed at this neglect of the Government, and I heard

the latter gentleman say that he had written a very plain letter to the Government, which he was then waiting a chance to forward.

Our ships had hemp cables in those days, and we had to keep them as straight up and down as possible by means of buoys, to prevent them being chafed by the shingle ballast thrown overboard by the Spanish merchantmen. This had accumulated in heaps in the anchorage, and the wisdom of Captain Phillip's order concerning this was shown by one of the transports neglecting it and nearly getting adrift, through the strands of her cable getting chafed through.

The *Sirius* was so cumbered up with stores on the gun deck that we were unable to salute the Spanish governor of the island—the Marquis of Brancéforte. We were at peace with Spain then, and so our Commodore had to apologise very handsomely for this apparent discourtesy.

I had never seen foreigners at home before, and I am bound to say they treated us with great consideration, and I left Teneriffe with a much better opinion of the black-whiskered Dons than when I entered it.

But the most notable event that occurred while we were here was this,—At daybreak one morning, when I was on sentry at the gangway, a boat from the *Alexander* came alongside, and an officer asked to be shown down to the Commodore. In a few

minutes we learned that a prisoner named Joseph
Powell had got away about midnight from the
Alexander, and had not been recaptured.

Just then my relief appeared, and I was going
below when I was ordered to keep under arms and
form one of a search party after Powell. Boats were
lowered, and a regular search of the shores of the
harbour began, two boats from the *Supply* lending
us a hand. It appeared that a boat had been left
hanging astern of the *Alexander*, and Powell by
some means had managed to get into her and cut
her adrift without being discovered; in fact, it was
not until four in the morning, when the guard was
relieved, that he was missed. Just astern of the
Alexander, a Dutch Indiaman was lying, and Powell
worked the boat over to her and offered himself on
board of her, but they would have none of him. He
got into the boat again, and was supposed to have
gone over to the west side of Santa Cruz.

With us in the boat was the master of the
Alexander, who was in a great state of mind over
the affair, for he was under a penalty of forty pounds
for every man that escaped. We could not but laugh
at him for the way in which he urged the rowers
to their work, and his constant lamentations about
his ill-luck. However, his troubles soon came to
an ending, for, as we rowed along the west side or
the harbour, the lieutenant of the guard on the
Alexander, who was in our boat, suddenly called upon

the men to stop, and we all turned our eyes to the land.

There, at the foot of a great rock which it appeared he had been trying for many hours to climb, lay the poor, hunted wretch, too exhausted to move, or even to speak. Quick as lightning the officer grasped my musket.

'Don't shoot, sir,' I could not help saying.

He took no notice of me, but levelling the piece, called out to the fugitive,—

'Surrender, you Powell, or I'll fire.'

Poor creature ! He did not utter a word, but merely turned his white, ghastly face, streaked here and there with blood, towards us, and the lieutenant, still keeping his musket at the present, the boat was rowed close in to the rock.

'Two of you get out and bring him into the boat,' ordered the officer, and myself and a comrade got out, and lifting him up carried him into the boat. I shall never forget the look of utter despair in that man's face ; it seemed to come from his very soul.

We took him on board the *Sirius*, where, on the following day, he was given twelve dozen and sent back to his ship, and kept in irons till we put to sea again.

While we were at Teneriffe, one of the convicts, who was a coiner, tried to practise his villainy, but met with swift retribution. It came about by reason of our seamen, who had taken very kindly to the fruit of the country, but had not the wherewithal to buy it, getting this dangerous rogue all the pewter spoons and other metal they could lay their hands upon. With this material the fellow made some exceedingly good imitations of the silver dollars of the island, and the sailors set about to pass them off on the island vendors, paying the coiner for his evil work with tobacco. But the very first attempt to pass the money failed, and the sailors, to save themselves, confessed the whole plot. Their grog was stopped by way of punishment, and the rogue was soundly flogged, suffering a double punishment, for he was cursed as well most heartily by the sailors and the prisoners for depriving them of their spoons to so little profit.

We only stayed a week at the island, and then the ships weighed and once more we were under full sail for our next port of call, which was to be Rio de Janeiro in the Brazils and, until we reached there, nothing of moment occurred, save that the *Supply* gave much trouble by the fearful manner in which she rolled and shipped great quantities of water. She could not carry much sail, even in moderate weather, for she nearly buried herself when on a wind.

CHAPTER X

ALL this time the fate of Mary Broad and Will Bryant was much in my mind, for, although when I had written to my father I had asked for news of the unhappy girl who had thrown herself away on such a worthless person as Will Bryant, he had in no wise answered my questions. But though I call Will a worthless man—as, indeed, he was when weighed against the girl—yet, as a man, he had many good qualities in his character, as will be shown.

As I have said, the last I had heard of the two was that Squire Fairfax was endeavouring to secure a reprieve for Will Bryant, and that Mary had petitioned to be sent to Botany Bay, and Lieutenant Fairfax had told me that it was likely her petition would be granted. I made many inquiries among the Marines doing duty in the transports as to whether a man named Bryant and a woman named Broad were among the prisoners they were guarding, but the

76

convicts being all known by numbers and not by
their names, no one could give me any clue to my
unhappy acquaintances. In the case of Bryant this
caused me no wonder, but I thought that Mary's
great beauty, were she on board, would easily make
her distinguished from her companions, and so at
last felt pretty sure that she was not with the Fleet.
I did not like to ask Lieutenant Fairfax anything of
the matter, for in those days discipline was very
severe, and for a private to venture upon familiarities
with his officer would have been most improper.

But one day, after we had left Teneriffe, the
lieutenant himself broached the subject. I was clean-
ing his accoutrements when he came up to me and
said quite suddenly,—

'Dew, did you ever hear what became of Bryant
and that poor girl, my sister's maid ?'

'No, sir,' I replied, 'but I should be very pleased
to know for certain that the girl was left in England.'

'I am sorry to say that she is, without doubt, on
board one of the transports. I had an opportunity the
other day to speak to the Commodore on this matter,
and he, kindly turning up his papers, found that
William Bryant and Mary Broad are both on the
list of prisoners.'

'God help them both, then, sir,' said I, and there
flashed through my mind the awful faces and vile and
blasphemous talk so common among the female convicts in the transports.

Then the lieutenant said, 'I had hope, Dew, when that fellow Powell got away at Teneriffe that it was Bryant, and, hang me! I should have been glad if it had been Bryant and he had got away. 'Tis a sad pity such a fine fellow should have met with such a fate.'

'Worse for the misguided woman who has thrown herself away on him, sir,' replied I.

The lieutenant fixed his keen, grey eyes on me for a second or two and then said quickly,—

'Yes, that is true. By the way, Dew, I think you were a little sweet in that quarter, eh?'

'That was long ago, sir, before I became a man and a soldier, and she would have none of me.'

I saw my dear master smile as he turned away his face, but the next instant his eyes met mine.

'Well, Dew, we must try to help better their condition when we get to Botany Bay. Only duty first, you know Dew. We must not let private feelings interfere with duty, my lad.'

'I believe, sir,' I said, 'and I am proud to say so, that you, sir, have made a good soldier for the King out of William Dew.'

'That's right, Dew. I am glad to hear you say this. Keep on as you are going. That will do, my lad.'

It pleased me very much that the lieutenant should talk so much to me, and that he took such an interest in my welfare. But yet it was a blow to me to hear that Mary was on one of the transports after all, with such depraved and wicked companions. I had hoped to the last that the authorities would not transport her, despite her petition.

We arrived at Rio de Janeiro on August the fifth, and once more the people of the Expedition were put upon fresh provisions, which was a great boon to us all. We had been at sea since May the twelfth, and during that time fifteen prisoners and one of a Marine's children had died. I heard Captain Phillip one day tell Mr Morton, the master of the *Sirius* (for he was most condescending to all his officers), that considering the dreadful condition of the foul and overcrowded transports, and the warm weather we had met with, that it was only by God's mercy that half of our human cargo had not perished miserably. During the passage, a great deal of rain fell, which would have caused more sickness, but that the surgeons frequently exploded small charges of gunpowder on the 'tween decks of the transports; and by this means, and a constant use of oil of tar, the dark, ill-ventilated prisons were kept in as good a state as was possible under such bad conditions.

Well, and now to Rio. Our Commodore had once served with the Portuguese, and, on the arrival of the Fleet, the town was illuminated in his honour and great kindness was shown to all our people, and besides this, our ships were excused from paying all dues to the port.

The Commodore here made purchase of all sorts of seeds and vegetables for use in the Settlement, and also acceded to an urgent request of our major for a supply of musket balls, the which, I can assure you, made our minds much easier. Almost one of the first things that our good Commodore attended to when we arrived was to convey ashore and see well cared for, the master of the *Sirius*, Mr Micah Morton, who had injured himself while we were unmooring ship at Teneriffe, and two midshipmen who had been ailing all the voyage. He was, in all that concerned the welfare of his people, a most kind and tender-hearted Gentleman.

During our stay at Rio de Janeiro, the *Supply*, which had been sailing badly, was altered in her rig; and then, embarking our stores, we took our departure for the Cape of Good Hope on September the twenty-first. The voyage across was a very rough one, and the *Sirius* rolled terribly, and our anxieties were increased by the carpenter discovering that the ship's waterways were in a rotten condition, and, indeed, so badly had she been fitted out by the rascally navy-yard contractors, that it is a wonder she did not roll her decks out, guns and all.

Between Rio and the Cape there was a plot formed on board the *Alexander* to seize the ship, but, providentially, it was discovered in time in a very simple manner. Some boxes of candles were found to have been broached, and one of the officers secreted himself in the hold, thinking to surprise the thieves on the next visit. He was hidden near the forward bulkhead, close to the crew's quarters, and, as he lay watching, he heard the men discussing a plot they had formed with the prisoners to seize the ship. Indeed, the villains had already stolen and concealed a number of crowbars, which were to be served out to the prisoners when the proper moment came to overpower the guard.

As soon as this was reported to the master of the *Alexander*, he signalled to the *Sirius* and, being to windward of us, ran down under our stern and hove-to while Captain Phillip dealt with the matter. This he went about very quickly. The ringleaders of the plot were seized and ironed to ringbolts on the deck, and four of the seamen were brought on board the *Sirius*, and their places taken by four of our men.

On the seventh of October, the master of the *Lady Penrhyn* signalled to the Commodore that a convict woman on board his ship had given birth to a son, and on the thirteenth day of the same month we arrived in Table Bay at the Cape of Good Hope. Here we obtained fresh provisions, and took on board the transports a great number of animals for breeding purposes at the new settlement. All these lumbered the ships up very much, and the seamen got to calling their vessels Noah's Arks. The day after we anchored, Mynheer von Graffe, the Dutch governor at the

Cape, a fine, soldierly-looking man, came on board the *Sirius*, and was pleased to say that we Marines were a fine body of men.

All being in readiness for our departure, the Commodore now determined to haul down his flag on the *Sirius* and go on ahead of us in the *Supply*, taking with him, among other officers, our commander, Major Ross. The brig was the fastest sailer in the fleet, and Captain Phillip thought to get on ahead of us, so that he might put the settlement in some sort of order before the main part of the expedition arrived. The *Alexander*, *Scarboro* and *Friendship* were ordered to try and keep up with the *Supply*, and a number of carpenters, surveyors and blacksmiths were selected from the convicts, and placed upon those ships. And now I come to what was the most affecting incident of this memorable voyage, and that was the meeting between Lieutenant Fairfax and Mary Broad.

As I have said, three of the transports were ordered to sail under convoy of the *Supply*, and this left the *Sirius* with the *Charlotte*, *Lady Penryhn*, *Prince of Wales* and the three storeships, the *Fishburn*, *Golden Grove* and *Borrodale*. These changes made it necessary to put some extra prisoners on the *Lady Penrhyn*, the complement of this transport being made up chiefly of females, but there were also a small number of men. On the day that this change was made, Mr Fairfax was on board of the *Lady Penrhyn*, taking over some papers from her marine officer who was going on with

the Commodore's squadron.   Mr Arthur Bowes was
the surgeon on this ship.

I was not present at what took place on this day,
but Mr Fairfax described the scene to me, and, as
nearly as I can, I will endeavour here to set it down
as it took place.

The master of the ship, Mr William Sever, Captain
Campbell and Lieutenants Collins and Fairfax and
Surgeon Bowes were in the ship's cabin talking over
matters of duty when the mate knocked at the door
and informed them that four female convicts and two
children had arrived alongside in a boat from the
Friendship, and that the sergeant of their escort wanted
to see Mr Bowes.

The surgeon went upon deck, and returning presently said to the officers who were chatting in the
cabin,—

'I have some more ladies given into my care.   I
shall begin to think that the Commodore has a high
opinion of my virtue if he sends me many more of
them.'

'Oh,' says Mr Fairfax, not knowing that Mary
Broad was among the women he was joking about,
'you need not boast of your virtue.   The women, if
all accounts I hear be true, are neither beautiful nor
virtuous, so that you are under no great temripta-
tion.'

'Come on deck and take a look for yourself, Mr
Fairfax, at one of my latest additions to the flock, and

I think you'll own yourself wrong as to their want of beauty.'

So thereupon they all trooped up on deck, laughing and joking. They came to the break of the poop, and looking down upon the main deck, they saw standing together in the ship's waist the women who were waiting to be disposed of by the surgeon.

'Which is your swan, Mr Bowes?' said my lieutenant, merrily.

At the sound of his voice, one of the women turned sharp round and looked up into his face. Then with a little cry she stepped a pace or two forward, and put her hands together as if she would crave a boon.

'By George, Fairfax! the girl knows you,' said Captain Campbell. 'I saw her jump at the sound of your voice.'

'Alas!' said my lieutenant, 'I know her well, poor girl, she was once my sister's maid,' and then, seeing them looking at one another in a very knowing manner, he divined what was passing in their minds, and added somewhat hotly, 'Gentlemen, you quite mistake the situation; the poor girl is as honest as the day, but 'tis her love for a notorious smuggler named Bryant, belonging to my native place, that has got her into this dreadful situation.'

Then he told them the sad particulars of Mary's history, and, being honourable men, they showed great sympathy for the poor girl. Mr Bowes, the surgeon, said he would see to it that her lot on the ship should be as comfortable as possible, and he would go and tell her so forthwith.

In another moment he was talking to the poor girl, and presently he beckoned to my lieutenant to come and join them.

As he came up to the group, the other women and Mr Bowes drew back so as not to overhear their talk.

'Mary, my girl, how have you fared?' said Mr Fairfax, and I well know how his kind tones must have wrought upon her woman's heart.

'Very well, sir, thank you. I have nothing to complain of,' said the girl, but yet her dark eyes glowed, and she clasped her hands tightly together, and her mouth worked. She was dressed in a very humble fashion, in some common woollen gown, with a shawl, such as all the prisoners wore, thrown over her black, wavy hair. But, despite the poverty of her attire and the dreadfulness of her surroundings, said my lieutenant, her great beauty shone out like as would a bright star in a sky of darkness, and there was the same fire in her eyes as in the old days when she set my heart a-throbbing on Solcombe Cliffs; indeed, all the suffering she had gone through in mind and body had not changed her ever so little.

For a moment or two she did not speak but gazed downwards to the deck, and then her voice came to her, as, with a sudden gush of passion, she laid her hand upon his arm.

'Charles Fairfax, you made love to me once, told

me that I was fitted to be a lady and offered to disgrace yourself and break your good father's heart by marrying me when you found I was no simple country wench to play with and then cast aside. Was there enough truth in your words to help me now? God knows how much you *can* help me.'

'Mary,' he began, when she placed both hands upon his arm, and, tossing her shawl back from her head, looked into his face with a very great expression of pleading misery.

'Mr Fairfax, forgive me. I am only, after all, a poor, weak woman, and I have done wrong to bring back to your memory words that I have forgotten long ago; but, sir, I beseech you, as an honourable gentleman and a King's officer, to do what I ask. You are the first man I have ever asked a favour of. Grant it me, and, perhaps, some day God may give me the power to show you my gratitude. Grant it, sir; Charles, for Heaven's sake, don't refuse me, or I shall go mad with suspense,' and then, although she did not weep, she shook and quivered from head to foot, and but that she held his arm would have fallen to the deck.

This laid the lieutenant all aback, and he hesitated a moment. Then said he, 'Mary, I was infatuated then, and your beauty made me make a fool of myself, as you say. Besides, you would have none of me. Bryant was, and is, the man you love.'

'True, indeed,' said the girl; 'I do love him in a

way that you fine folk know nothing of. But only my good sense saved you from linking yourself to me, and at least you owe me gratitude for that,' and with that she drew back from him with a proud look.

'Tell me what you want, Mary. I have sufficient regard to do anything for you consistent with my duty, but you know that it was your own wish to come with this—'

'Oh, heavens,' and a swift gleam of fire came into her eyes, and her voice grew marvellously hard, 'don't preach to me. Do you think that I want to go back with what I have begun? All I ask of you is that you will speak to that fool of a surgeon, or the head jailer, or whoever is your master, and get me sent into the same ship as my Will is on.'

'What good can that do, Mary, we leave here in a day or two, and then shall see no land until we reach the settlement, so that if you hope to escape—'

'Escape! I have no such thoughts, but cannot you see that I, who have gone through so much that I might some day speak to Will again, am eating out my heart in waiting for that time, and that even to be on the same ship with him would help me to bear the rest with patience, even though we might not speak together,' and again her voice grew tender, and ended in a sob.

'Very well, I will try to do what I can, but I don't even know what ship Bryant is in.'

'Neither do I, but, oh, Mr Fairfax, for the sake of

those days gone never to return, try all you can to do this for me ; ' and then, said my lieutenant, one, but only one, tear fell upon his hand.

' I will, Mary, I will do my best,' and then he said with a laugh so as to cheer her up, ' Good-bye, Mary, I suppose you know the name of the place where we now are, don't you ? '

She smiled back at him. ' God bless you, Mr Fairfax. I have *good hope*, indeed, now.'

Then the lieutenant turned away, and the surgeon spoke to the girl and told her to behave herself and he would do what he could for her.

Mary replied in a very humble way, and then, with her fellow prisoners, went below.

The lieutenant told all that had taken place to the others, and then for the first time learned that Will Bryant was on board of the *Charlotte;* the strange part of the matter was that he had actually been transferred to that ship from the *Lady Penrhyn* the previous day, to take the place of a carpenter who was going on with the commodore. As so many women were on the *Lady Penrhyn*, it had been determined to take the few men out of her and thus reduce the chances of a mutiny and the need for so strong a guard, some of the Marines being put on board the *Charlotte* where there was a great number of male prisoners.

After some further talk in the matter, Mr Bowes and the others said they would not object to Bryant being returned to the ship if Mr Fairfax would mention it to the Commodore, and obtain his consent, and to that end my lieutenant sought to put himself in the way of Captain Phillip before the *Supply* sailed.

CHAPTER XI

A MARRIAGE SCHEME IS ARRANGED WHICH DOES
NOT ALTOGETHER MEET WITH MY APPROVAL,
AND WE ARRIVE AT OUR DESTINATION.

It so happened, that on the very day of the meeting between Mary Broad and my lieutenant, that Captain Phillip dined in the ward-room with all the officers who were not actually on duty, for we were to sail the next day, and it was always his kindly nature to associate as much as possible with those under him and join in their conversation, and this he did without in any way sacrificing his great dignity and courtesy of manner.

After dinner, he explained over some wine what were his intentions immediately after the expedition landed in Botany Bay, where he expected to arrive some time in advance of the rest of the fleet, as, although the whole of the ships were to get under weigh together on the morrow, Captain Phillip thought that the *Supply* and the three transports with her would far outsail the rest of the fleet. Mr Fairfax was not present, being then at the time on the *Lady Penrhyn*.

I was in attendance at the table, and my heart jumped to my throat when I heard the Commodore utter these words,—

'One of the first things to be attended to after the landing will be the pairing of some of these unfortunate females with suitable male prisoners. Heaven knows, gentlemen, we need to encourage morality among them, and I propose to marry as many couples as possible. There are not enough single women or widows to go round with the number of single men, but I daresay we shall be able to procure native women who will be willing to mate with the male prisoners we cannot provide with European wives.'

The only chaplain we had with us was Mr Johnson, and he was a Methodist, and I felt sure it was he who had put this matter into the Commodore's head.

Said Captain Hunter, 'And how do you propose to sort out all these precious couples, sir ? '

When the Commodore first put his idea before his officers, it did not give me a great shock, for, thought I, this will come in well for poor Mary who has come so far for the sake of the man she loves, but the next words of Captain Phillip, in answer to Captain Hunter's question, quite took me aback.

'I think the fairest way will be for them to draw lots,' he said.

'A devilish good idea,' said my officer, Major Ross,

and I could have struck him for saying it, although he was my superior, and a good officer.

'Better let me pick them out according to their physical fitness,' suggested Dr White, the chief surgeon to the expedition.

'That is a good idea, doctor,' said Captain Phillip, gravely bowing to him and raising his glass.

'I should think, sir, that it would be well to leave this matter as much as possible to me,' said Mr Johnson. 'If it be necessary, sir, to pair off these lost creatures like cattle, pray let me, who will have to perform the holy ceremony of marriage, endeavour to find out the spiritual condition of some of them, and by a judicious selection make good citizens of them.'

The officers tittered and one or two laughed outright, for none of them loved the parson, but the Commodore's voice made them cease.

'The chaplain is right, gentlemen. I shall form a committee of selection, to consist of Mr Johnson, the doctor and myself. By this means we may, out of very bad material, breed some very good subjects for His Majesty.'

Then there was more talk of what was to be done, and we who were waiting at the table were told that we might leave the ward-room, and so I heard no more, but I determined that Mr Fairfax should be told what had taken place directly he came on board, in the hope that this off-hand marriage scheme might be so

arranged as to benefit rather than injure the unhappy
pair in whom we were both so painfully interested.

Accordingly, when the lieutenant returned, I took
the first opportunity of telling him all about the
matter, though I was by no means sure how he would
take such a liberty on my part.

'Why, Dew,' said he, 'this is very singular. I
must see the Commodore at once, whatever comes
of it.'

It was then that he told me of what had taken place
on board the transport, without, of course, entering
into all those particulars I have given in my diary—it
was long years afterwards that I learned all the circumstances of the interview. The lieutenant at this
time merely informed me that he had seen Mary
Broad, and that she was still infatuated with Will
Bryant, and was anxious to make the rest of the
voyage in the same ship as he was.

'Which,' said Mr Fairfax, 'I have promised to ask
the Commodore to consent to.' The lieutenant did not
ask me for my opinion, and so I dared not say anything,
but I must say that I could see that no good could
come out of such a matter, but I held my peace,
and my betters decided the thing wisely enough without me.

So Mr Fairfax got leave to go off to the *Supply* that
afternoon, and, having the consent of Major Ross to
interview the Commodore on this matter, and Captain
Phillip being willing to see him, he was shown into

the little cabin of the *Supply* and told his story and what he wanted in as few words as possible. Long afterwards, I was told all that took place, but on the lieutenant's return he sent for me and said, 'Dew, my lad, the Commodore has refused to put these two on one ship, but has promised that they shall be among the first couples married as soon as we arrive. That will do, let us hear no more of the matter.'

With this I had to be content, but I afterwards heard what took place. Said the Commodore, 'This is quite a romance you tell me, lieutenant, but, from what you yourself say, Bryant and this woman are scarcely the persons to put on board the same ship. Either one of them has spirit enough to attempt an escape, and this woman, by your own showing, is a prison breaker. No, I cannot have that.'

'As it pleases you, sir,' answered the lieutenant, 'but may I entreat you to interest yourself in these unfortunate persons' future?'

'Sir, pray understand I interest myself and feel deeply for everyone of these people, and I cannot undertake to separate any one or any two of them from their fellows in such poor endeavours as I am capable of towards effecting their reform.'

'I quite understand that, sir,' answered my lieutenant, who was a little ruffled at what he thought was an unnecessary reminder that his personal feelings must be smothered where duty was concerned, 'but I understood you had some idea of arranging for the marriage of some of these people, and—'

'Quite true, Mr Fairfax, and this suggestion of yours shall receive every consideration, 'tis reasonable enough'—and here the gallant gentleman placed his hand on the lieutenant's shoulder with a kindly smile—'that this man and woman should be married to each other, if the circumstances of the case are as you understand them. In fact, I will promise you that, if the chaplain and the doctor find no fault with the arrangement, this Bryant and the young woman Broad shall be the first couple I will have spliced when the pairing off begins.'

My lieutenant thanked the Commodore, and returned to the *Sirius*, and the next day, which was the thirteenth of November, the whole fleet got under weigh again, and on the twenty-third we had cleared the land, and the *Supply* and her convoy had parted company.

The routine was now the same as before, except that we had a great deal of bad weather and sighted many large whales. In the bad weather, the *Prince of Wales* lost a man from the main-yard when snugging down one night, and no little damage was done to the sails of the convoy.

On January the second, we saw for the first time the long-looked-for land. This was the South Cape, which years afterwards was found to be an island and was named Van Diemen's Land.

From this point we shaped our course for Botany Bay, and again made the land on January the nineteenth, seventeen hundred and eighty-eight, and standing off and on during the night for the convoy to come up, we entered the bay on the following day, and found the rest of the fleet waiting us.

CHAPTER XII

BOTANY BAY

To-day I have reached the allotted age of man's life, and I know that presently, when I enter the best parlour, I shall be welcomed by many dear faces ready with kindly greetings and affectionate tokens, to remind me that my seventieth birthday is not forgotten by the loving hearts about me.

How different it all is in this year of our Lord 1834 to that time forty-six years ago, when our storm-beaten and battered ships, with their cargoes of sin-stained and suffering humanity, dropped anchor off the wild shores of Botany Bay.

Since then that settlement, the first seeds of which were sown amid the sighs and groans and tears of the wicked and worthless, and the swish of the dreadful cat and the clank of iron gyves upon weary limbs, has become a free and flourishing colony, and the memories of the sad past are well-nigh forgotten. And indeed, though I did see much that sickened me of the swift and stern punishment that was the fate of

G

these evil-doers who sought to renew their crimes in a new land, and though some of those in authority were cruel and heartless, yet do I honestly believe that most of those who were then my superiors were good and conscientious men, who sought to do their duty to their country and their King. And I shall ever take pride, my dear children, in the thought that it was my honoured lot to serve under such men as Captain Arthur Phillip and Captain Hunter and Lieutenant King; for not only were these gentlemen good officers, but they were better—they were good and clean-living men amid all that was wicked and vile.

Since those days, Captain Hunter, Colonel Collins, and Captain Tench and Mr White, our old surgeon, have written full accounts of all our early sufferings and misfortunes and the ups and downs of the brave hearts who, in spite of endless adversities of famine and shipwreck, made good their footing upon those distant and then savage shores.

But there, this journal of mine is no place to record those moving adventures and strange events, and I make no pretensions to write a history of the settlement, for in truth I really took but very little part in the colony's history after our arrival, being one of a party of Marines told off to remain on board the *Sirius* to act as a small reserve.* Thus it is that

* The reader is referred to the Introduction by the Editors. As a matter of fact, much of Sergeant Dew's journal has been here omitted, as the matter can be read in any history of New South Wales.

much that I have here set down I learned from my comrades, who were doing duty on shore.

It was on Sunday, January the twentieth, that we sailed into the bay, and then we learned that the *Supply* had arrived on the previous Friday night, while the transports had only got inside the previous evening, so that the brig had not so greatly out-sailed us after all.

Lieutenant King, the second lieutenant of the *Sirius*, Lieutenant Dawes of our detachment, and the Commodore, who had gone on in the *Supply*, had landed directly the brig was at anchor, and begun exploring the shores of the bay for a suitable site for the settlement. The land disappointed them, for it was very much like an English moor, and dull and unpleasing to the eye for the most part. They saw some natives, quite naked, but these were peacefully inclined, and though rather timid at first soon began to make friends with our people. But although so timorous of our people, they yet fought very fiercely among themselves; for soon after our landing at Port Jackson, the Governor was a witness to a battle fought among themselves, which shows they are not lacking in courage. Captain Phillip was exploring the northern side of the harbour, near the entrance, when he saw this encounter, and the brave way the natives fought so impressed the Governor that he named the little bay in which this matter happened, Manly Cove.

A further examination of the shores of Botany Bay made the Commodore so dissatisfied with the place that he resolved to make a boat expedition to the northward, and examine Broken Bay and Port Jackson—two bays sighted and named by Captain Cook.

On the twenty-first, the *Sirius* and her convoy having got safely to their anchors, the Commodore, with Captain Hunter, the judge-advocate (Mr Collins), and the masters of the *Sirius* and *Supply* set off in three boats to examine the coast north, while Mr King and Mr Dawes had orders to search the shores of the bay for good fresh water, the want of which was the Commodore's chief objection to forming the settlement at this place. Meanwhile, however, a party of the prisoners were set to work clearing an open space of ground, so that, should the Commodore decide to remain, a beginning would have been made.

We on board the *Sirius* were not allowed to lose time waiting, for our people were employed getting up cases of saws and such like implements, in making seine poles and getting fishing gear ready. A saw-pit was made on shore by a party of the prisoners, but before it was finished the order came to knock off and bring the gear on board.

On the twenty-third the commodore returned, and we soon learned that Port Jackson, about nine miles to the northward, had been fixed upon for the settlement. On the twenty-fifth the *Supply* weighed, having on board a party of our men and some fifty convicts. She got in the same night, and the next morning at daybreak the Jack was hoisted on shore and the land taken possession of for His Majesty, our men firing a volley, and the officers drinking the health of the King.

Before sunset the same night the transports and the *Sirius* had also anchored in the harbour, and I saw for the first time the place of the new settlement. The site was at the head of a cove on the larboard arm of the bay, which is full of inlets and is a fine, safe harbour. Just at the head of the cove a clear rivulet empties itself, and the soil, though thick with trees and rocky near the shores, seemed to us very fair.

On the twenty-seventh the convicts and our men were landed and encamped on the west side of the stream of water, and the Governor and the principal officers, with a guard, were encamped opposite to them.

I must not forget to mention that, just after the *Supply* left Botany Bay, two French ships which had been cruising about trying to get in, made the port. These were *La Boussole* and *L'Astrolabe*, commanded by Monsieur de La Perouse, and bound on a voyage of discovery.

They had been unfortunate in their voyage, as we afterwards heard, having had some of their officers massacred by the savages of the islands they had visited.

Our Commodore sent some of the officers to visit the Frenchmen, and they went round to the bay in our ship's cutter, and I believe took some dispatches which the foreigners said they would deliver when they got back to Europe, and we took some dispatches of theirs to send to England by the first ship.

Long afterwards we heard that they never reached home again, and their fate to this day has never been discovered, though it is supposed that when they left Botany Bay they foundered in a gale.*

* The unfortunate La Perouse and all with him were, it has since been ascertained, lost on the island of Vanikoro.—EDITORS.

CHAPTER XIII

I TAKE A SMALL PART IN A VERY IMPORTANT CEREMONY

I WAS landed from the *Sirius* to do duty with the main guard on the Governor's side of the Tank Stream in Sydney Cove—as it was afterwards called, in honour of Lord Sydney, though there was some talk at first of calling the settlement Albion.

Day and night for a week, when not on sentry duty, I had to remain close to the guard tent, for in it were placed the colours of the detachment, which Major Ross had had trouble enough, as he said, to get permission to bring with us, and which had to be guarded. Besides the pair of colours there were many important boxes, containing papers, ammunition and the like, and the guard tent was the rallying point in case of a mutiny, or of an attack by the natives.

In the bustle and excitement of the first week after our landing, I saw nor heard nothing of Will and Mary.

Only some of the prisoners had as yet been landed, and these were at work on the other side of the Cove, felling the great trees and erecting rough huts and tents in readiness for the general disembarkation, while no women were allowed on shore for the first week. But on my side of the stream the live stock and plants and seeds were landed, and stock was taken of our possessions. It was then found that we had four mares, two stallions, four cows, one bull, one bull calf and a few sheep, poultry, goats and hogs, all of which Captain Phillip had bought at the Cape.

On the afternoon of Tuesday, February the fifth, five women were landed and escorted to our side of the Cove, and as I saw them coming towards where I was keeping guard, I thought one of these might be Mary Broad. But she was not among them, and it afterwards turned out that these women were destined for Norfolk Island, whither Lieutenant King was bound in the *Supply*.

However, on the following day, all the ships' boats were got out, and by sunset that night, every prisoner in the fleet was landed and encamped. When all were on shore a muster roll was called, and it was found that from the day we left England until our arrival, the number of deaths of all parties in the expedition only numbered forty-eight.

It was a very dreadful night, for before the tents could be properly secured, an awful storm came upon

us, with such thunder and lightning and rain as I
had never dreamed of, and man as I thought myself
to be, my heart was filled with fear. Many of our
live stock were killed by the hurricane, and Major
Ross lost five sheep, in which he took great pride,
but I confess I was not sorry to lose them, for I
had been given the charge of them, and they cost
me much trouble by straying away, and I feared to
meet with natives when searching for them.

Lieutenant Fairfax I had seen very little of during
this first week on shore, for the Governor, as we
now took to calling our good Commodore, had found
him a great deal of work surveying the ground, he
being much skilled in this science.

There was terrible work that night among the
depraved characters who were landed, and I shuddered
when I heard afterwards, from my comrades doing
duty on that side of the Cove, of the fearful scenes
which they had witnessed, when I thought that Mary
was among the women who, 'twas said, had led to
all the riot, although, poor girl, she had nought in
common with the vicious wretches by whom she
was surrounded.

The next morning at ten o'clock everybody belonging to the settlement was assembled on the banks
of the little rivulet, to hear Governor Phillip read
his Commisson.

We Marines were all under arms, and only one
sentry was left at the guard tent. Our colours were

unrolled, and our drummers and fifers played good music as we fell into line.

The prisoners were all drawn up at a short distance, and then the Governor, and all the officials of the settlement, and our regimental officers and the ships' officers, assembled in front of us.

A camp table stood handy, and on this were a lot of papers, which Mr Collins read out in a clear voice. These documents were the commissions of the Governor and our commandant (who was appointed lieutenant - governor), and Mr Collins himself, who was the judge - advocate ; the parson and the surveyor-general ; all had their commissions read also, and everyone was much impressed with the ceremony.

The Governor very prettily thanked the detachment for its services, and then he ordered the convicts to sit down, as he wanted them to pay attention to what he had to say.

Then it was that among the crowd of abandoned felons I saw, for the first time since I had left England, Will Bryant and Mary Broad. They were seated together holding each other's hands, and seemingly quite indifferent to all that was going on about them ; and I saw that every now and then the girl would let her eyes dwell lovingly upon the face of the man for whom she had dared so much.

I learnt afterwards that this was the first time they had met since leaving England. The male

prisoners had been marched on to this parade ground
from our direction, and the females from another,
and then, for the first time, many of the men and
women recognised among their fellow-exiles some old
acquaintances.

Mary and Will were, strange though it seemed,
but little changed from when I saw them last, and
the girl looked pleased and happy, as if forsooth
'twas something to be proud of to be in such a
situation.

They did not see me; the girl was too much
wrapped up in her lover to have eyes for any but
him, and as for Will, he held down his head, and I
thought looked as if he felt awkward and ashamed
at being so taken possession of by a woman.

Presently, the convicts all being seated on the
ground, Captain Phillip, in a clear voice that could
be heard by every soul present, addressed them, as
nearly as I could remember when I wrote the
speech in my journal, in these words. Said he :—
' Prisoners, I have given you a very fair trial during
the passage out, and I have had some of you working under my own eye for the last week, and I am
sorry to say that I think many of you are incorrigible
and case-hardened rogues, that nothing but severity
will induce to behave properly. Make no mistake
about it,' and here his voice grew terribly hard and
stern, ' if the scenes of last night are attempted to
be repeated, the guard has orders to fire upon you,

to put a stop to your riotous debauchery. Therefore, for your own sakes I implore you to take heed.
Out of some six hundred of you who ought to work,
not more than two hundred have shown an inclination to do so. Very well, I will take care that the
industrious shall not labour for the idle—those who
do not work shall not eat. In England, thieving
poultry is punished with death, and there poultry is
plentiful. Here a fowl is of the utmost consequence
to the settlement, for they are reserved to breed as
well as every other species of stock ; therefore, understand me, whoever steals the most trifling article
of stock or provisions shall be punished with death.
It will be grievous to my feelings to exercise severity,
but the welfare of all demands most rigid execution
of the laws.' He stopped for a while, and then
resumed, in a milder tone : 'The work you will be
called upon to do will not even equal the labours of
the husbandman at home, but everyone of you must
and shall do your share towards making the community prosperous. And we shall begin by erecting
comfortable dwellings for the officers and men of the
Marine detachment, and afterwards suitable houses for
yourselves.'

Then the Governor spoke in still kinder tones, and
reminded them that the greater number had already
forfeited their lives to their country by their wickedness, but by the leniency of His Majesty's Government they were given this chance to redeem their

characters, and he would do all he could for those who deserved his clemency.

Then he concluded by saying, and you may depend upon it that some of us paid strict attention to his words :—'I propose, as a means of settling some of you in a comfortable manner, that such among you as appear to wish it, and as are suitable, shall be lawfully married, and begin a new life respectably.'

After this we fired three volleys, and all the officers had dinner with the Governor. The detachment was marched back to the cheering sound of drums and fifes to its encampment, and the convicts to their rough huts and tents.

CHAPTER XIV

WILL BRYANT AND MARY BROAD ARE MARRIED

THE next day or two went by quickly enough. The prisoners were set to work at building, and our detachment was occupied in guarding them.

One afternoon Lieutenant Fairfax came to the guard-tent where I was on duty.

'Dew,' said he, 'I am afraid you can no longer act as my servant. The Governor says we are to have convict servants in future, and that the red-coats are wanted for duty.'

'I have spoken to the Governor,' went on the lieutenant, 'and Mary Broad and Bryant are to be married next Sunday.'

'It is about time they were, sir,' I replied. 'May I make bold to ask if you saw how the young woman behaved herself last Thursday when we were paraded?'

'Oh, yes, I saw them, and I saw nothing to find fault with in Mary's behaviour. She has shown that she is deeply attached to Bryant, and 'twas natural enough she should be pleased to see him. What fault have you to find with her for that?' and he wheeled about and faced me.

'No fault, sir, if you think her conduct becoming in a modest young woman,' said I, somewhat timidly.

'Look here, Dew, my lad, I am afraid that you are a deuced sight too virtuous and easily shocked in matters of love-making to understand such a woman as Mary. I am quite certain that no young woman of your choosing will ever get transported on your account.'

I saw that the lieutenant did not half like my boldness in having been so free with my opinions, so I only saluted by way of reply.

But Mr Fairfax was only putting me in my proper place, as I, having more sense now, well understand, and he was by no means annoyed with me, for he went on,—

'I am going exploring for some days directly, and I sha'n't have much opportunity of seeing you. Remember, Dew, do your duty like a soldier and a man, as you have been doing, and you will get along all right. I have spoken well of you to the officers, and 'tis likely that they will not forget my recommendation. That will do, Dew, for the present. Good-bye.'

'Good-bye to you, sir,' said I, and was about to salute again when he caught my hand and shook it, saying,—

''Tis no crime against military law to shake hands with an honest comrade, so let us shake hands first

and salute afterwards, then all will be according to
Cocker.'

Then he slewed on his heel and walked off, leaving
me very much affected by his good-natured condescension.

On Sunday, February the tenth, the Reverend
Richard Johnson held divine service under a big tree,
the detachment and all the prisoners being paraded to
hear the service read.

Then after the service Mr Collins stepped to the
front and read from a piece of paper a list of men and
women who were to be married, and the first two
names he read out were Mary Broad and William
Bryant. When their names were read out, Mary and
Bryant stepped forward, and Mr Fairfax, who was
standing with a group of officers near the Governor,
smiled encouragingly at them, and the girl's face
seemed to me to suddenly grow more beautiful than
ever, as her eyes lit up with an answering smile, but
yet could I see that her whole frame was shaking like
an aspen leaf.

The Governor said a few words in an undertone to the
parson, and then he turned to the lieutenant and said
something to him, and the lieutenant saluted, and I
could see he was explaining to the Governor that these
two were the prisoners on whose behalf he had spoken.

Then Captain Phillip bade Will and Mary approach
closer to him, and he spoke to them in a kindly way,
but not so quietly that we could not hear what he said.

'You, Bryant,' said he, 'and you, Mary Broad, I
have determined shall be the first couple married in
the settlement. Lieutenant Fairfax has spoken to me
about you, and has told me your history. He says I
can take his word for it that you will turn out good
settlers. I hope you will justify the interest he takes
in you, and that you especially, William Bryant, will
remember that in the love of this young woman you
have a very sheet-anchor to hold you to a life of honest
endeavour and good conduct. I shall take you to be
a very poor and paltry fellow, indeed, despite your
bodily strength, if you go to leeward with such an
incentive to a good life as I believe this girl Mary
Broad will prove. Now, Mr Chaplain, proceed with
the ceremony.'

Will Bryant held up his head, saluted the Governor,
and spoke up like a man.

'God bless your honour. You may rely upon it,
sir, that I will do my duty, and that Mary here, my
wife that is to be, will make me as good a man as you
have among us prisoners.'

'It will go hard with you, sir, if she does not make
you a better,' answered Captain Phillip, quickly, but
still I saw he was pleased with Bryant's words.

And then Mary, not a whit abashed, although her
hands shook and her bosom heaved as she spoke out so
that we could all hear her, said : 'And I thank you, sir,
too ; and I thank Mr Fairfax for this good act. But,
sir,' and here her black eyes flashed and sparkled as in

H

the old days, and one hand stole out into Will's, ' but, sir, we are not criminals but as honest as any man or woman here, bond or free.'

' Tut, tut, girl,' said the Governor, somewhat impatiently—for how was he to know that Will and Mary were different from any other law-breakers—and I half-feared he would get angry and knock the ceremony on the head at once, but my lieutenant again said something in a low voice to him, and then he smiled, and said,—

' Well, well, I know no distinctions at present, but plenty of distinctions will be made in the future as people by their conduct deserve them. Smugglers, thieves, and all the rest of you make a fresh start from to-day. Now, Mr Chaplain, go ahead and splice them. You know there is a long list of names to go through yet, and we have no time for speech-making over each couple.'

Then the parson solemnly read the service, and a ring which was lent by the Governor himself for the purpose was used for the ceremony, but the parson only put it on the woman's finger and took it off again and made it go the rounds, and then returned it to the Governor.

Our commandant, Major Ross, made a little joke of this, about the danger of letting such people see gold rings, and the care the parson took not to let it out of his hands.

But the Commodore soon put a stop to this. Said

he, 'No, no, major, no joking, please. These people have feelings, you know, and it is not necessary or seemly to be always reminding them of the past.'

And so Mary Broad became Mary Bryant, and as I was marched off from the parade ground I felt that I had quite got over any weakness I once had in that quarter.

CHAPTER XV

IN order that I may get to that part of my life's experiences which I wish to relate fully, it is necessary that I give but scant account of what happened in the settlement up to the month of October, in the year 1788, when I left it for some months and made a voyage to the Cape of Good Hope in the *Sirius*.

As I have said, Lieutenant King was dispatched in the *Supply*, with stores and implements of all kinds, to form a settlement at Norfolk Island, a very fertile spot situated about three hundred leagues from the mainland; it being in the Governor's mind that the island would grow crops for the main settlement, where the soil was not so good as it was at first thought to be.

Mr King took with him Mr Cunningham, the master's mate of the *Sirius*, Mr Thomas Jamison, surgeon's mate, Mr Roger Morley, an adventurer who had been a master weaver and had volunteered for the expedition to teach the people how to weave flax, which it was thought would thrive well on the

116

island, two Marines and one seaman from my ship,
nine male and six female convicts.   All the convicts
selected were men of good build and strength, for it
was thought that, besides their other labours, they
should cut down some of the tall pines growing on
this island, which might serve to supply masts to ships
calling at Port Jackson in the future.

The *Supply* sailed out from between the headlands
of Port Jackson on February the fifteenth, and on the
seventeenth discovered and named an island after the
first Lord of the Admiralty — Lord Howe.   This
place, though small in extent, is yet of some fertility,
and is about one hundred and thirty leagues from
the mainland.   Although barely two leagues in length,
the south end rises to a great height, and about ten
miles away is a vast, pyramidal rock, which was named
after Lieutenant Ball, who commanded the *Supply*.
The expedition arrived safely at Norfolk Island, and
the brig returned to port on the nineteenth of March.

Our settlement now began to show signs of progress.   The married convicts, for the most part, were
industrious, and the Governor had given to each couple
a small plot of land to cultivate, and the Bryants, so
I heard, were getting to be well liked for consistent
efforts and steady industry.   The country all around
the cove being so poor, a farm was begun at a place
called Rose Hill, some miles up an arm of the waters
of. Port Jackson ; a fine brick house was built for the
Governor, and a hewn-stone hut for the lieutenant-

governor ; store-houses were also built of stone, and a barracks for our men was begun ; meanwhile, both we Marines and our prisoners had to lodge in roughly-made huts. Each of our officers was allowed a grant of two acres of land and a convict labourer to cultivate the soil.

Soon after we landed there began a serious difference between our commandant, Major Ross, and the Governor, about the duties of the marines, and the people in the settlement took sides in the matter. The trouble came about in this way. One of my comrades, Private Joseph Hunt, struck another, named Will Dempsey, and was tried by court-martial. The sentence of the Court was that Hunt was either to ask public pardon before the detachment of Dempsey, or receive one hundred lashes. The major regarded this sentence as contrary to military law, because it gave the prisoner a choice of punishments, and ordered the Court to alter the sentence, and this the Court refused to do. Then Major Ross ordered the officers of the Court under arrest, and as they were wanted for duty the Governor tried to square the matter between the major and his officers. The officers held to their sentence, and the major held to it that he would have them under arrest, and so, after some weeks of pursuasion, and finding that no good came of it, Captain Phillip ordered the officers to return to their duty. This was the beginning of the trouble between the military and civil authorities, and it lasted till the detachment returned to England, and was a source of great worry and vexation to our good Governor during his time of office, to see men that he liked personally at loggerheads. Major Ross knew his duty, and was perhaps a little sensitive about the dignity of the detachment. He did not, for instance, like the notion of our men being employed as gaolers; but Captain Phillip considered that it was our duty to help push on the work of building by seeing that the prisoners laboured hard. Our major thought our duty was simply to form an armed guard for the defence of the settlement, against mutiny on the part of the convicts or attacks by the natives. Captain Phillip also wanted our officers to form part of the civil Court, but they did not consider their commissions entitled them to act in such a capacity. Another cause of ill-feeling was, that the Governor thought it wise to form into constables the better behaved of the prisoners, and some of these fellows had the impudence to make prisoners of some of the men of the detachment, and Major Ross was, as I think he well might be, very indignant about it.

The prisoners were a miserable lot of creatures, who knew little or nothing of agriculture, and less, if possible, of the useful building trades and such like arts, and so we progressed very slowly in these things, and suffered many hardships.

We were constantly trying to make friends with the natives, who seemed harmless enough but very stupid. They were quite naked and had no habitations, except for a kind of screen made of the bark of trees, which they erected as a protection against the wind and rain, and under the lee of which they lay down. They seldom appeared in numbers exceeding twenty or thirty, and they lived chiefly by fishing. Their only arms were clubs and roughly-made spears and a kind of curved javelin, which they could throw in such a clever manner that it would describe a circle in the air and return to them. Although they were, as a rule, terribly frightened of our firearms, yet they were by no means to be despised, on account of their treachery, and, indeed, the Governor was actually badly wounded by one of them, who threw his spear at His Excellency with unerring aim; but yet, Captain Phillip would never revenge himself upon the savages.

There were no wild beasts or other monsters to add to the terrors of our position, except very ferocious sharks, with which the waters of the bay were infested. There was one curious animal, called a kangaroo, which walked and leapt upon its hind legs in a very diverting manner, and there were hundreds of bright-coloured parrots.

Notwithstanding the Governor's expressed determination to put down vice with a strong hand, one of the sailors of the *Alexander* was caught in the women's tents a day or two after our formal landing, and the rascal was drummed out of the camp with his hands tied behind him, our drummer playing the 'Rogue's

March,' and one of our own men was given one hundred lashes for the same offence.

I must not forget to mention that the first settler was a prisoner named James Ruse. To him the Governor lent thirty acres of land, at a place called Parramatta; this was in November 1789. This man married and had one child, and being a very industrious man was able to support himself in a year or so; whereupon His Excellency, being greatly pleased thereat, granted him the land as his own, and it was formally deeded to him on February the twenty-second, 1792, under the name of Experiment Farm.

CHAPTER XVI

SHOWING HOW A ROGUE LED CAPTAIN PHILLIP TO
LOOK FOR GOLD,* AND HOW MATTERS PRO-
GRESSED AT THE SETTLEMENT.

THE convicts—or at least the greater part of them—
were sad rogues, and it became necessary to flog and
hang many of them before they could be got in any
sort of good order. A week after we had landed, the
triangles were rigged, and a few days later a gallows
was put up just within cry of the little town we had
made, and we soon had occasion to use them ; indeed,
hanging was the only cure for some of the wickedness
that throve apace in the settlement ; as for flogging,
they seemed to take but little account of that, and
would take the risk of it with great cheerfulness,
by committing all sorts of petty thefts and such
rogueries.

Not long after the expedition had landed there
began to be some talk of the country containing gold,
and indeed I had heard much of this on the voyage out,
for many persons in the expedition had said that it was

* Gold was not discovered in Australia until many years after
Sergeant Dew was dead.

likely that gold would be found. Perhaps this was
because that there were among us, people whose
ancestors could remember the talk about the South
Americas in the days when every adventurer strove to
reach that part of the world where it was supposed that
gold abounded ; and so, in one way or another, the
idea we had taken into our heads when we were very
young got about among us again, that the metal was
to be found in every unexplored country. Of course,
too, the convicts, who always kept their ears open,
soon grew to talk about the matter as well as the freemen, and we soon had an example of how one of the
rogues made use of the common belief that gold was
in the country. This fellow was a man named Daly,
a big, bony Irisher with cunning, grey eyes. He had
been transported for coining, and was a most incorrigible villain ; and after I left the colony was hanged
for breaking into the Government stores.

Well, one day up comes this fellow to one of our
officers with a piece of metal resembling gold, and a
story that he had discovered the place where it lay in
astonishing quanties. If, he said, with many a twist
and roll of his villainous eyes, his Honour, the
Governor, would obtain his pardon and send him home
with a certain female prisoner with whom he was
intimate, he would reveal its whereabouts. He told
this story with such a truthful air that he was believed
by the Governor himself ; or at least Captain Phillip,
when Daly was brought before him, treated him with

so much consideration that the rascal was inclined to brazen the matter out.

I was one of two Marines told off, as an escort over the man, to take him to Captain Phillip, and I heard all that took place.

Said the Governor, ' Now, Daly, my man, tell us all about this great discovery of yours and we will see what we can do for you.'

Then the fellow, pulling his forelock, and looking as demure as a village rustic in spite of his rogue eyes, answered that 'twas true he had found gold, and that he had sold some of it for good coin to a gentleman belonging to the *Golden Grove*.

Then the Governor had a general muster and ordered the fellow to point out who 'twas that he had sold the gold to. But this he could not do, yet, notwithstanding, persisted in saying that he could point out the spot, so an officer and twenty men—I being one of them—were despatched with him in search of the place. After going about ten miles into the bush the fellow suddenly bolted and we had a great search for him, but could not find him, and returned to the camp, where the rascal was discovered sitting upon a log and laughing at us.

Major Ross then ordered us to seize the man and lash him to the triangles, and the Governor told the major to flog him until he confessed the truth. It took three hundred lashes to bring him to reason, and between every hundred he was asked to own that his story was a lie, but he stuck to it until the three hundred, and then confessed that he had lied from the beginning and that his only object was to lead the Marines on a wild-goose chase and fool our good Governor.

As time went on, our detachment became very discontented with the situation, for the Marines were now treated by the Governor with great severity for the slightest breach of discipline. A prisoner who struck a Marine was only punished with a hundred and fifty lashes, while a Marine who was found in one of the women's tents was given a hundred lashes ; so there was much grumbling, but our officers were good and loyal men, else their would have soon been a mutiny, for they too were much discontented.

The first execution took place in February, when James Barrett, a prisoner, was hanged for stealing from the Government stores. This seems a very dreadful punishment for such an offence, but I will say for Captain Phillip that he was a very mild man and neither hanged nor flogged these rogues unless they richly deserved it, and he had often warned them of their fate if they stole food ; but notwithstanding this, before I left the settlement in October many rascals were swung at the gallows, and flogging had become quite common.

In May my old master, Lieutenant Fairfax, returned to Sydney Cove from a long excursion into the country to Rose Hill, where he had been superintending the erection of an observatory and the laying-out of the principal farm of the settlement.

By his good exertions on my behalf I was promoted to the rank of corporal, and considering the short time I had been in the Service, I had good reason to be, and was, very proud of the honour, I can assure you; and my comrades envied me much. I was promoted in the place of the corporal who was in charge of an island which was close to the settlement, and where a garden had been made to grow vegetables and such like produce for the use of the *Sirius* and *Supply*. The place was called on that account Garden Island. The corporal in charge and a seaman were severely punished for grievously wounding a comrade in a quarrel, and these men's misfortunes led to my advancement.

The Governor about this time hit upon an idea to punish lazy prisoners instead of flogging them. There was a small rock near the entrance to the cove, which we called Rocky Island, and on this, when a man would not work, he was placed for a week on bread and water until he came to his senses, which, as he was alone and was not allowed more than a bare ration, did not take long, and he dared not try to swim back on account of the ferocity of the sharks. Rock Island on this account soon came to be called Pinchgut, and the device of the Governor proved very effective. I ought to mention that the Governor did not forget to keep up the King's birthday, and a whole batch of rogues who were to be hanged in that week were pardoned, so that they might have cause to remember His Majesty's goodness.

After a while, as we began to get fairly settled down, the transports left one by one for England, and soon the *Sirius* and *Supply* were the only ships left in the cove. Before leaving, the masters of the transports hove them down and overhauled them, and Captain Hunter told the Governor that the frigate— for so he called the *Sirius*, though she had little claim to that title—would have to be served in the same way, for her hull was in a very bad condition, and when at sea and rolling badly, the timbers in her top-sides opened and shut in a very alarming manner.

Our farms at Rose Hill and on the shores of the settlement were not yet of much benefit to us, and rations were beginning to run pretty short, and the Governor began to get anxious, as soon as it became evident that our first year's crops would come to no good, all the seeds having got heated and spoiled on the long voyage. It leaked out, too, that Captain Phillip had expected a supply of stores from England soon after our arrival, and was now somewhat despondent, believing that the Government at home took but little heed of our necessities.

As for Norfolk Island, our hopes in that direction were all well enough for the future, but of course Mr King could not be expected to send us supplies for many months to come ; and so it came about

that the poor, old, battered and worn-out *Sirius* had
to be despatched to the Cape of Good Hope to bring
us stores for the settlement.

The fishing, which we had hoped would have
helped us so much, also turned out a failure, and the
great shoals of fine, large, pink-coloured fish with
bony foreheads, which at first were plentiful in the
Cove, and were especially thick about the small rocky
island which we afterwards called Pinchgut, suddenly
left, and nothing but hungry sharks seemed to fill the
waters of the harbour. Then, in addition to our many
other troubles, the Indians, as we then called the
black native inhabitants, began to get troublesome, and
I cannot but help thinking that much of this was
brought about by the good-nature of the Governor, who
would not suffer them to be treated with anything but
the utmost kindness ; and when, as was often the case,
one of our men or a prisoner was injured by them,
and took a just revenge, the Governor always punished
the white man ; for, said he, ' I have seen enough of
these people to know that they are a mild-tempered,
innocent race, and I am convinced that they must
have received provocation before they would do any
of you an injury.'

All the same, there is no doubt in my mind the
savages of this country are a treacherous race,
and I will give you one instance of their murderous
inclinations.

On the thirtieth of May two men were cutting

and gathering rushes at a bay near the settlement, and as they did not return at the time appointed, a party of our men was sent out to search for them. Their bodies were found in the bush, quite dead and with many of the spears of the natives sticking in them. The savages had carried away the rush-cutters' tools. I knew these two fellows to be quiet, inoffensive prisoners, as I had often guarded them at work. The Governor himself, with a squad of our men, went out to try and find the murderers, and by-and-by he came upon a party of them, but he refused to punish them, saying that he was sure they must have had some provocation and the best way to treat them was to teach them better, and so he merely made signs to them that such conduct was very wrong.

This was, of course, humane treatment on his part, but I agreed with our major's opinion as I had often heard him express it, that it would have been better to have been a little more lenient with our detachment, and expended more powder and shot on the savages.

As soon as it was decided to dispatch the *Sirius* to the Cape, and she was got ready for sailing, her crew took up their quarters on board, but some of the officers and a few handy men, such as carpenters' mates, were to be left behind as useful to the settlement.

The Marine afterguard, the Governor thought, ought to be left behind, but as it was necessary by the regulations that the ship, being one of His Majesty's

I

frigates, should have some Marines on board of her, it was decided that four privates and a corporal in charge should accompany the ship for guard duty, and very proud was I when I learned that I was to be the corporal selected for this important post.

By this time our settlement had grown into quite a big town as towns go, for it consisted of over a thousand persons, and so you can easily understand that there was not much intercourse between the Marine detachment and the prisoners. We were forbidden to make friends with the convicts, and all the self-respecting men among my comrades had little to say to the men and women prisoners.

For these reasons I had not seen anything of the Bryants, and had no wish to renew my acquaintance with them, especially as my position had so changed that I had to be very careful not to jeopardise my superiors' good opinions of me. However, just before I embarked on the *Sirius*, Lieutenant Fairfax had a conversation with me on this matter.

CHAPTER XVII

MERIT REWARDED

I WAS, indeed, very proud the day that saw me made a Corporal of Marines, but I take pleasure to think that I bore myself with all due modesty. The lieutenant was good enough to congratulate me upon my elevation.

Said he—'Good-day, Corporal Dew, I am glad to hear of your promotion.'

'Thank you, sir,' said I. 'I hope to do my duty as a non-commissioned officer as well now as in the days when I was of more humble rank.'

'I am sure you will,' replied the lieutenant, 'only, Dew,' and here he placed his hand on my shoulder, 'only try and be kind to the privates under you; remember you were once a private yourself, you know.'

The kind manner in which this was said brought a lump to my throat, and at first I could find no words to answer him.

Then he laughed quietly, and I had some idea that

he was making fun of me, though I could see little enough to laugh at in my new responsibility.

Presently he said, 'Have you heard or seen anything of your friends, the Bryants?'

I thought this was scarcely the way to speak of such persons, but I answered, 'No, sir; of course, I have no intercourse with prisoners, it is against the regulations.'

'Oh, no; of course, I might have known that you would not break a regulation of this kind,' and I thought his grey eyes flashed quickly, 'but their position has been greatly improved of late. You see, the Governor, learning that Bryant was a good boatman, has put him in charge of a fishing party, and it is hoped that he may be able to get some fish out of the Cove where less experienced men have failed.'

I guessed at once that this was the lieutenant's doing, and I thought it was very good of him to take so much interest in people of this description. So I remarked that I hoped these persons would recognise the leniency of their treatment.

Then the lieutenant suggested that it would perhaps do no harm if I were to say farewell to the Bryants, and if I cared to do so, he would give me a written permit to visit them in their hut.

I did not relish the idea very much, but Mr Fairfax seemed to think that my elevation might perhaps serve as an example to them that good conduct was not overlooked by our superiors, and so I said with a good grace, that if he thought it right, of course, I would go over and see them.

Accordingly, the Sunday before we got to sea, after church parade, I walked over to the Bryants' quarters.

Port Jackson contains many little bays and inlets, Sydney Cove being almost at the head of the harbour. On the east side of the cove there is a regular row of bays for the whole way to the southern headland, a distance of about six miles. In the first of these bays, next to Sydney Cove, our town farm was made and we called it Farm Cove ; it was here that the Bryants' hut was situated and the fishing boat was kept.

When I got to the hut, Will Bryant was sitting outside the door on the grass, mending a seine net, and as I approached him he rose from the ground and advanced to meet me.

At Solcombe, the last time I had spoken to him, he was a fine, stalwart, young fellow of about six or seven-and-twenty, and looking his age and no more. In those days, scarcely two years gone by, he was as straight as a musket-barrel, and he looked you in the face with his light blue eyes in a way that told you he was as honest a man, smuggler though he was, as any in the village. Then he had fair, curly hair, and kept himself cleanly shaved and smart-looking, as such a properly-built young man should do.

In the few times that I had seen him since we had landed, it was always at a distance, or I was too much occupied with looking at his wife to take much notice of him, and so I saw in him but little change; but now that I was thus brought face to face with him, I saw that he was no longer the Will Bryant I had known at Solcombe.

He was clad in the coarse, canvas clothing which had been served out to the prisoners, and which was all of one pattern, and stamped the men who wore it as being different to their fellows. Instead of the clean-shaven, well-cut features and crisp curly hair that had made a good-looking fellow of my old acquaintance, he now wore a grizzled beard. His hair looked as if it had not been combed for many a day, and his face was roughened and grimy, and there was a strange, hardened look in it.

'Good-day to you, Bryant,' said I. 'I hope that you are pretty comfortable, and that your wife is well.'

'Good-day to you, Corporal Dew,' he replied. 'I am sure it is very good of you to ask. I am doing well, as well as I deserve, no doubt, being nothing but a common felon. My wife is well, our rich fare and gentle life, with all the comforts it gives us, you may depend, agrees with her. And what, may I make so bold as to ask, has brought you to visit us to-day? 'Tis something like two years since you have spoken to me.'

'Oh, I only came to wish you good-bye as an old

acquaintance ; I am going away in the *Sirius*.   Of course, we have not spoken to each other since you got into trouble ; circumstances are different now to what they were at Solcombe.'

'I am sure it is very good of you to be so condescending, Corporal Dew.   Here is my wife ; no doubt she will appreciate your kindness.'

Then Mary came out of the hut, and looking at me very straight in the face, she said, 'And what might you want, William Dew ? '

'I merely came to say good-bye, Mrs Bryant ; being old acquaintances, I thought you might like to say farewell, as I am leaving in the *Sirius*.'

'Oh, indeed.   I thought you had said good-bye to the like of us before—long before—'

'Yes, when I got into trouble,' said Bryant, looking steadily at me.

'Yes, when William Dew and yourself got into trouble, and his skin was saved, thanks to you,' said Mary.

I felt there was a bitterness in this meeting, and I thought it would have been better not to have brought it about.

'I suppose you are coming back with the *Sirius*, and so you will have another opportunity, when you are made sergeant, of showing how well you are doing.   Good-bye, I wish you well,' said Mary ; and then she just gave me her finger-tips and a flash of her black eyes and went inside the hut again.

'You must forgive us, Mr Dew,' said Bryant. 'We are strange, perhaps, to you, but then, you know, things are not what they were, and you are in a different position to us now.'

I began to feel that somehow I was not showing to advantage, and that, perhaps, I had forgotten too readily how easily I might have made one of the prisoners betwixt whom and myself I was so ready to draw nice distinctions. Besides, I had begun to see that if Bryant had been less generous, and had not put the whole blame of my share in our smuggling adventure upon himself, he might have suffered less, and I might not have escaped scot-free. And so a feeling came over me that made me extend a hand to Bryant and say, as I turned to go away,—

'Good-bye, Will. If anything that I can do in the future will benefit the little one as yet unborn, remember, that Corporal of Marines though I am, the child will have a friend in me.'

Will Bryant pressed my hand, and before he could say some words that I could see he was struggling to get out, but which somehow he seemed too much upset to utter, I walked rapidly away to my quarter of the settlement.

Once only did I happen to look back, and I saw him standing where I had left him, with his hands clasped together and his face bent to the ground; then Mary came out from the hut, took his hand in hers as if he were a child, and led him inside.

CHAPTER XVIII

I WILL not here weary you with all the details of our
voyage in the *Sirius* to Table Bay and back, save to
say that before sailing we had to land eight of our
guns and much of our shot to lighten the old craft
and make room for the stores we were to bring back,
and when we sailed out from Sydney Cove we saw
Lieutenant Fairfax mounting these guns on a redoubt
at the west side of the Cove. Our voyage was a very
wearisome one, for the old ship made very bad weather
of it, and soon after leaving Port Jackson the scurvy
broke out among our crew, and three seamen were
buried at sea. This scurvy is indeed a most dreadful
and malignant sickness, and the spectacle of our suffering crew filled me with horror and dread. Then,
later on, we sprang a leak and we were heartily glad to
cast anchor in Table Bay after so perilous an experience. As soon as we got to speak to the people of the
place we heard that some of the transports on the way

137

home to England had come to grief, and we thought
we were well-to-do in having escaped shipwreck ourselves, for our sailors said the old ship was so rotten
that they feared the voyage back, and many would
have deserted but that we Marines kept too strict a
guard upon them.

On the twenty-second of February we set out on
our voyage back, and on the night of the nineteenth
of April, when off a little island about twelve miles
from the coast of Van Dieman's Land, we were nearly
lost in a fierce, southerly gale ; indeed, so perilous was
our position that Captain Hunter said to the second
lieutenant, who had succeeded Mr King,—

'This is beginning to look serious, Mr Fowell. We
are making lee way very fast and the land must be
close to. Bear a hand and repair the storm mizen
staysail, and get it and the reefed foresail set.'

'Ay, ay, sir,' said the lieutenant, 'but I fear, sir,
that the foresail, instead of lifting her rotten old carcass
to the sea, will only bury her into it.'

'We must do it, however, Mr Fowell,' said the
captain, in his quiet way. 'The men are getting
nervous, and we must give it to her.'

So for three hours the old *Sirius* plunged madly into
the mountainous seas, every now and then huge green
seas toppling over the waist and filling her decks, and
all hands stood by and looked out to leeward in fear
and trembling, for already we could discern the black
loom of the land. And all the while Captain Hunter

stood aft near me and my men who were at the reliev-
ing tackles at the rudder, and spoke words of caution
and encouragement to us.

I shall never forget the horrors of that night, but I
shall always remember with pride that whenever I
looked at the features of our brave captain as he came
near the binnacle light, that my heart seemed to grow
suddenly big, and that all fear seemed to vanish from
within me. Once Mr Fowell came and spoke to him,
and said,—

'What will they do for stores now, sir, at the
settlement ? '

The captain placed his hand on Mr Fowell's
shoulder. 'God help them, indeed, if we go ashore ;
their necessities are very great, and I pray that we
may get out of this mess for their sake.'

For this was the nature of this good seaman and
honourable gentlemen ; he ever seemed to think of
every other person before himself; indeed, hot and
short-tempered as he was sometimes, he was yet a
man beloved by all on board the *Sirius*.

But it pleased the Almighty to save us that night,
for after a while we managed to get the mainsail and
another staysail set, and although she plunged and
reared like a maddened horse, and great seas continually swept over the waist and into the cabins, yet she
dragged through it somehow, and when daylight broke
we saw that we had just weathered a high, rocky headland which lay about half a mile away from us.

Then, although we had escaped so far, we had yet to undergo a further terrible experience, for although we kept a great press of canvas on the ship to work her off the land, she strained and laboured so heavily in the truly awful sea that Captain Hunter thought all hope of saving her was past. So fierce and resistless were the huge waves which every now and then leapt bodily upon the decks and swept everything before them, that the condition and appearance of the ship was most pitiable to look at. All that day we struggled hard along the savage-looking coast line, upon which the surf beat with astounding fury, and not for one moment did Captain Hunter leave the deck, although his officers besought him to take a little rest. About midnight the wind shifted a couple of points to the southward, and we began to work off shore a little, the ship still staggering madly along under a great pressure of canvas, and every now and again taking huge seas over on the starboard side. That night was indeed a dreadful one, and when daylight broke through the black, lowering mist to the eastward, we saw that we were still close to the shore. Then our hearts failed us, especially when, a few minutes afterwards, some of the crew seeing the sea breaking heavily all around us called out that we were among the breakers, and the helmsman became so frightened that he threw the ship up in the wind, and sea after sea crashed down upon the poor old vessel, and fairly buried her for a few minutes. But after a

while she freed herself, and Captain Hunter, seeing
that there was not room to wear, stood on, and in
another hour or two we saw that the land began to
trend to the northward, and the sea moderating a
little, the captain kept the ship away a point, and
although she rolled terribly and still shipped monstrous
seas, she steadily worked off this forbidding coast, and
we breathed again, thankful to the Almighty for His
mercies. From that time the weather steadily improved and the wind hauled to the southward, so that
on the morning of May the eighth we once more saw
the headlands of Port Jackson, and in the afternoon let
go our anchor in Sydney Cove.

So heavy was the press of canvas we had carried
during that terrible gale, that the figurehead was
washed away, and the head rails and knees of the head
were so much damaged that we were obliged to get
lashings round the cutwater to secure it to the stem.

When we entered the Cove we presented such a
shattered appearance that the ship was not known.
When they found out who we were they gave us a
warm welcome, for soon after we sailed the flour had
run so short that the allowance to each person was
reduced by a pound a week, and this was restored on
our arrival.

CHAPTER XIX

SOME DESCRIPTION OF OUR TOWN AND THE SORE STRAITS WE WERE IN FOR FOOD

ALMOST as soon as the anchor was down we, the Marine guard of the *Sirius* were relieved by some of our comrades from the settlement; for Captain Hunter had sent word ashore that we were quite done up and worn out with the hardships of our terrible passage.

The first news we heard was that a comrade of mine, named Tom Bullmore, had been killed in a fight with some of our men, and four of the Marines had been tried and sentenced to two hundred lashes each for the crime. Jim Rogers, another Marine, and a very respectable, quiet man, had been lost in the woods somewhere near the rush-cutters' cove, and his remains were never found, although great search had been made for him; some supposed that he had been captured and killed by the savages.

A great deal of work had been done in our absence, and I will try and tell you what our town looked like.

The country round about the settlement was called

Cumberland, after the Duke of Cumberland, and its
boundary in a westerly direction was at Rose Hill,
where our principal farm was situated. At this place
a number of prisoners were kept at work, and a
country house had been erected for the Governor.
An officer and a company of Marines did duty in
this wild and lonely place, in spells of three months
about.

In a northerly direction the Governor had explored
as far as Broken Bay, but no settlement was formed
there. To the south Botany Bay was our limit, and
there a fishing party was stationed to help eke out
our provisions.

On the southern headland, at the entrance to Port
Jackson, Mr Southwell, a master's mate of the *Sirius*,
was stationed with a small party, and their duty was
to keep a lookout for the arrival of store ships, which
we were now anxiously expecting from England.
They had built a few huts and a lookout place, and
erected a flagstaff, and with this and one of the
guns of the *Sirius* they were to signal arrivals, but,
alas! nothing had arrived for them to signal.

The old *Sirius* rode at anchor close to the mouth
of the harbour, and the *Supply* was moored on the
west side near a cove in which we had, before sailing
for the Cape, hove the old ship down. Near the
headland, on the north shore of the harbour, were
fixed our scientific instruments, and this we called
the Observatory. Then on the west side of the

Cove were the hospital buildings, and a main street was surveyed and laid out near here, its direction being about south-west from the shore. Barracks and temporary huts were close by, and also a prison for the ill-behaved.

On the east side of the cove the Governor's residence was placed, and near to it the main guard. A quarter of a mile inland were the officials' houses and our officers' quarters, and then beyond were more huts for prisoners. The workshops were near the prisoners' huts, and then on the outskirts of the settlement was the magazine. The triangles and the gallows were erected outside of all, up towards the head of the stream of fresh water, and not far from this was a burial ground. In the next cove towards the east was a small farm, and the fishing party to which Bryant belonged was hutted there.

A number of the Marines had brought their wives and children with them, and these married men's quarters were near the huts of the best class of married prisoners; but, as you may well believe, the wives and families of my comrades had too much self-respect not to keep well apart from the felons. Yet it was in somewise hard for the children, as I remember the wife of one of our men telling me that some of the convict children were as well trained as any in the settlement, but she, for one, would never let her children so much as speak to a felon's child. This was because two of a prisoner's children had

sought to join in some childish game with her
children. I could not but commend her for her
caution, although, as I have said, it bore hardly upon
the innocent offspring of both free and bond.

The daily work of the settlement was carried on
with very proper regularity, and we were a busy
community. In one place you would see a party
cutting wood, in another a blacksmith's forge blazed
and smoked, in another a gang of prisoners would
be dragging stones for building purposes, and at short
spaces you could everywhere see the bright coats
and glitter of the muskets and bayonets of the
Marine sentries on guard over the prisoners at work.
Then, every now and then, Captain Phillip would
be walking quickly about, looking at this or that
gang as they worked, but never saying a harsh word
to any one of them ; indeed, some of them had so
far gained his confidence that they had been appointed to supervise gangs of their fellows.

Bryant, I soon learned, had been given charge
of a gang told off to fish the waters of the Cove,
and he had behaved himself well, and was well
liked by his superiors. I also heard that a boy-child
had been born unto him, which he and Mary had called
Emanuel, after one of our officers who, with my
lieutenant, had shown much interest in them.

All this time, however, the stores were steadily
running short, although the *Supply* had twice brought
us a little from Norfolk Island, where Mr King had

made good progress, although there had been an attempt at mutiny there. The *Supply* had, on both voyages, taken down more prisoners, and the guard being small, the villains thought to overpower them. But Lieutenant King was not the man to be trifled with, and he soon put a stopper on that sort of work.

By-and-by matters came to such a bad pass for the want of provisions that six men of our detachment robbed a public store, and were speedily hanged for it; it was a terrible punishment, for we were all suffering sore temptation through our great hunger.

At last Captain Phillip, despairing of the arrival of the store-ships from England, determined, as Norfolk Island seemed to be flourishing, to send a part of our community thither; and to that end the *Sirius* and *Supply* were got ready for sea. Two companies of our detachment were embarked under Major Ross, who had orders to relieve Mr King, who was to return to the settlement.

I was sorry that once more I was to be separated from Lieutenant Fairfax, who was to remain at Sydney Cove while I took up my old station on the *Sirius*, though I was not sorry for the trip, as, when we left, I was on the books of the *Sirius*, and not in the detachment told off to remain at Norfolk Island. Our numbers were made up of sixty-five officers and men, with five women and children from the detachment and the civil department, and one hundred and sixteen male and sixty-seven female convicts, with twenty-seven children. This would, on our arrival, bring the numbers on the island to civil and military and free people, ninety; male convicts, one hundred and ninety-one; female convicts, one hundred; and children, thirty-seven.

We got under weigh on March the sixth 1790, with orders to return to Port Jackson as quickly as possible, for we were to voyage to Batavia for supplies. The day we left, the Governor put every adult person in the settlement, without excepting any one person, including himself, upon a weekly ration of four pounds of flour, two and a half pounds of pork and one and a half pounds of rice.

So away we sailed for Norfolk Island, little knowing what was to befall us there.

CHAPTER XX

WE made a fine-weather passage down to the island, the appearance of which my comrades and myself liked mightily, for its great greenness and profusion of rich verdure was very pleasing to the eye ; but yet it was sad to think that a spot of such beauty, endowed, as we afterwards found, by an all-bountiful Providence with the choicest gifts of scenery, climate and fruits of the soil, should so soon be turned by man into a veritable hell, and, as one of my officers said, disfigured by crime, loathsome vice and misery.

We were lucky enough to land most of our passengers on the fourteenth of March, when the wind began to blow with much force, and then we had to stand off and on till the nineteenth, landing the remainder of the people as best we could, together with the light baggage.

There are but two or three landing-places on the island, the best being at Sydney Bay and at Cascade Bay. The latter bay is a very beautiful place, the

148

shores being fringed with pleasant-looking clusters of richly-foliaged trees, over the tops of which tower great giant pines ; but in the interior the prospect is still more beautiful, and in places the country re-sembles nothing so much as some of the great parks in the south of England. Sydney Bay is on the south side of the island, and there is a very ugly coral reef here which shows its jagged teeth very plainly when the tide is out. About a league from Sydney Bay is a small, high island which was named Phillip Island, after our Governor.

Almost touching the mainland there is another island separated by a deep, narrow channel, and shaped somewhat like a horse-shoe, the open part facing to the east. In height it is about seventy feet, and in length, perhaps a third of a mile, and this, too, was covered with a thick, dense verdure of small trees. I have been told that, some five or six years after I left Norfolk Island, there came several very severe earthquake shocks which greatly terrified the inhabitants, who, on looking towards this little island, saw that part of it, nearest to the mainland, subside with a violent commotion under the sea, so that the channel was increased to half a mile in width.

The main island appears a precipitous spot, rising with great abruptness from the sea and furrowed by deep, storm-worn channels along its densely-wooded sides. To land at Sydney Bay the boat has to pass through a narrow passage in the reef I have spoken of, and the landing is altogether very dangerous.

We landed most of our people at Cascade Bay, and some of the baggage, but none of the provisions, and Captain Hunter began to get greatly worried, for he knew that the stock of food on shore was but little, and that the people would soon suffer hunger, if the weather did not take up and enable him to get some of the supplies to them.

The *Supply*, having oustailed us, had managed, she being a much smaller ship, to get into Sydney Bay, and anchor without much difficulty ; and so being, as I have said, fretful and anxious about the straits of those ashore, Captain Hunter determined to venture in close with the *Sirius* rather than box about to and fro off the island and perhaps get blown away altogether. The breeze being strong, he soon worked the ship close into the land, and then brought to, head off shore, and got out our boats and began loading them.

After the boats had sheered off, the wind began to drop a little, but there was a very heavy sea, and the captain saw that the ship began to set very much to leeward. Most of the crew being away in the boats, we who remained were at once set to get sail on her. But, notwithstanding all that we did, it soon became apparent that the ship could not weather the reef, and then, too, the wind shifted a couple of points against us, and she broke off in an

alarming manner. Captain Hunter at once threw
her in stays, but she missed, and made a stern-board ;
but, providentially, the current carried her just clear
of the breakers. Had we struck just at that part of
the reef not a soul would have lived to tell the tale,
for the sea was rolling on the jagged rocks with
astonishing noise and fury. Once clear of the
point of the reef, we filled again, and then brought
to the wind on the other tack, but the ship still
drifted fast towards the shore, and another attempt
was made to stay her ; this, too, failed, for the poor
old ship was very much out of trim, and we could
see by the weary, slow manner in which she came
to the wind that she would never go off on the
other tack. The moment the captain saw there
was no prospect of her staying, he gave the order
to let go all sheets and halliards, and our starboard
anchor was let go, but before it reached the bottom,
the ship struck with violence on a jutting ledge of
the reef.

It was my first experience of the kind, and the
dreadful noise and great shocks that followed each
other with alarming quickness very much terrified
me at first. The first time time she struck, the
rudder was torn away from the stern-post, and then
for a moment or so she hung by her heel on the
reef, with her stern high up and her bows so deep
down that the sea poured in over the head and filled
her decks to the waist.

In a few seconds, however, she lifted again to another huge roller that seemed to tower up far over the fore-yard, and then she was hurled, still stern up, farther back upon the reef, and then settled down with a terrible crash, bilging in the whole larboard side like a rotten egg-shell. Most fortunately for our lives, the ship's bows were head on to the seas, which now dashed over her with incredible fury, otherwise, so huge were the rollers that had they struck us broad-side on, we should have been capsized and rolled over and over like a log. In a few minutes after first striking, a great green wave leapt bodily upon her, and, lifting her forward, swung her round somewhat; she gave a frightful roll to starboard, and the fore and mainmasts went by the board, followed presently by the mizzen.

Encouraged by the example of the captain and master and other officers, our crew sprang to the work of cutting away the wreckage of the masts from the ship's side with a will, for there was a terribly strong back-wash, and every moment we feared that the great mass of masts and spars would be swept back over our decks again by the retreating waves and kill or maim every soul on board. I can well remember—so often do the veriest trifles at such times prove a matter of future interest to one's memory—that just as the main deck, from the terrific rolling, began to work loose, the master called out to those upon it to come aft to the quarter-deck, which he knew was safer, 'for,' said he, 'do you fellows think you are going to wait till the ship rolls her deck out so that you can all get ashore in it comfortably? Lay aft here, you lazy dogs.'

Now, thought I, if the master can make a jest out of such a terrible situation as is ours, why should I, who know nothing of shipwrecks, be in any way afraid. So this gave me good courage, and from that moment my alarm ceased. However, within a few minutes I saw the wisdom of the master's banter, for the ship gave another heavy roll to starboard, and I saw a great gape begin to show on the larboard side between the deck and the bulwarks, and soon after the whole main deck worked right out of her and was washed away.

By this time the people on shore, under the guidance of the officers of the *Supply*, had managed to get a line out to us, and bent a hawser to it. Our end of this we bent to the stump of the mizzenmast, and the shore end was made fast to a tree. Having plenty of men ashore, they soon got a whip and traveller to work, and then Captain Hunter, calling upon three of our ship's boys, sent them ashore one after another. One of them, being terribly frightened at the look of the seething surf through which he had to pass, clung to Captain Hunter's legs, but the master grabbed him by his slacks, lashed him securely for his trip, and he was dragged through and landed on shore nearly dead with fright and exhaustion.

It took us nearly two hours before we were all landed ; many of us, including Captain Hunter, were badly hurt in being hauled ashore, but yet, seeing that it had pleased God to spare our lives, none of us grumbled at our bruised and torn bodies, but rather thanked Him that we had any bodies left with enough life left in them to feel our bruises or wounds.

That night we were well cared for by those on shore, and, although I was very sore and stiff when I arose in the morning, I was yet determined to do my duty like a man. The weather was now moderate, and the surf no longer beat with savage fury upon the reef, and we saw that the ship still held together. Soon after mid-day an attempt was made to save some of the provisions, and two prisoners went off by the hawser to throw some of the live stock, such as sheep, fowls and pigs, overboard, and so give them a chance to swim ashore.

Certainly these rascals did throw some of the animals overboard, and then very quickly made their way to the cabin and got drunk, and there they remained until the evening, when they roused themselves, lit all the lamps they could find and then burst open the spirit room and made merry. By-and-by as the wind died away we could hear the

villains singing and laughing with much hilarity,
and Major Ross, seeing that there was every chance
of these fellows setting the ship on fire, called for
volunteers to go off and toss the rogues overboard.

Thereupon I offered, and a young prisoner, one
John Ascott, joined with me, and we were hauled
off on the hawser, and not a moment too soon were
we, for one of the after cabins on the larboard side
—that which had been occupied by Major Ross—
was already on fire. We soon managed to put this
out, and then turned to our two gentry, who were
both lying down upon a pile of cushions in a very
comfortable manner in a drunken sleep. Although
Major Ross had told me to throw them overboard,
I ventured not to fulfil this order, as he did not
take it into account that they would be too drunk
to move ; so we dragged them on deck, made them
fast to the whip and they were hauled ashore in no
gentle manner by my comrades, who were sore
over the grog being drunk by two such villains.
Then Ascott and I followed.

As soon as we were landed, we reported ourselves
to Major Ross, who awaited us in company with
Mr King and other officers. Ascott, he made a
free man for his good conduct on the spot, but
merely told me to go and change my clothes and
take a few hours' rest.

The next day, however, he sent for me and said,—
'Corporal Dew, you have always done your duty

like a good soldier, and last night I consider you earned a good reward. You have not been long in the Service, but your future rank is that of Sergeant.'

That was the proudest moment of my life.

CHAPTER XXI

WE SPEND A WEARY TIME ON A LONELY ISLAND

THE old ship held together for another day or two,
and we Marines assisted the sailors and prisoners to
save a good many of her stores and provisions ; then
it came on to blow again, a long, sweeping roll came
in from the southward, and in a few hours great curl-
ing seas flung themselves upon the battered hull, and
then we saw the last of the poor old *Sirius* reduced
to a few heaps of wreckage dashed upon the rocks of
Sydney Bay.

There is no doubt but that our major was a very
different kind of man to Governor Phillip ; and, without making so bold as to draw comparisons between
them, Major Ross was, perhaps, too much of a soldier
for the kind of work we were performing, besides
which, he was a man of very hasty temper, which
oft outran his judgment.

The very moment almost that the *Sirius* struck the
reef, our drummers on shore beat to quarters, and the
commandant proclaimed that the island was under
martial law.

A meeting of the major and Captain Hunter and Lieutenant King was held on the next day, and a proclamation was then made, that there being no civil court on the island any crime would be punished with death, and this was necessary to prevent theft and a general mutiny, perhaps, as well. We were assembled to hear this proclamation read at eight o'clock in the morning on the day after the ship-wreck.

The Union was hoisted on a flagstaff near the landing-place, and our detachment was drawn up in two lines, leaving a space in the centre for the officers. The *Sirius's* crew were in the rear of one line, and the prisoners in the rear of the other.

Then the drums beat a rally, and the colours which we had brought on the ship, on account of having the senior officer with us, were unfurled. The major read the proclamation, and then said he,—

'Officers and men of the civil and military detach-ment, you have heard the law of the island read, see that you observe it. Our position is a serious one, and I give you fair warning that it will be my duty to enforce, with the utmost severity, the penalty for infringement of the regulations.'

Then turning to the convicts he went on,—

'As for you, be honest, industrious and obedient, and all will go well with you, but' (and here his face darkened visibly, and the row of felons behind the line of Marines craned forward their heads to catch every word he uttered) 'but take care how you offend. I will have no mercy on idlers or plotters.'

Then we all gave three cheers, and every person, beginning with the major, passed under the Union flag, taking off their hats as they passed it in token of an oath to submit to the martial law which was thus proclaimed. And so began our life on this lonely island under the rule of the stern and dreaded major.

The *Supply* was despatched on the twenty-fourth of March to Sydney Cove to let them know what had happened. She arrived there on April the fifth, and caused great misery by the news she brought. Lieutenant King went back to Port Jackson in the brig, and I heard one of the prisoners tell a comrade who worked with him that the very worst behaved of them was sorry that he had gone and left them to be dealt with by the major.

Hearing this dangerous sort of talk, I threatened the fellow, who, however, was very humble and said he meant no harm. 'You see, sir,' said he, 'the lieutenant kept us from going to the triangles, and only sent us there when we deserved it, but the major follows us about with them.'

Now I ought to have had this fellow reported for his talk, but somehow his manner was so respectful that I overlooked it. And, indeed, we were all sorry to see the last of Lieutenant King, who, while he was very severe upon evil-doers, was very just to all who did their duty. When he arrived in Port Jackson, he was

ordered to England by Captain Phillip with despatches
reminding the Government of the great urgency of
sending us aid.   Mr King went by way of Batavia,
to which place the *Supply* was sent for food on the
eighteenth of April.

For eleven long, weary months we remained at this
place, and those months, despite the great beauty of
the island and the constant round of duty that gave
me but little time to fret, were the hardest to bear
that I, with even all the sad experiences I had undergone, have suffered.   You must know we lost many
things in the wreck of our old ship, all our energies
being devoted to saving what was likely to be useful
to us all in common, and so many of us went short of
clothes and other comforts.   My duties while I
remained on the island were to take my turn with
the other sergeants in charge of a squad of Marines
who watched the prisoners at their work upon the
roads, the buildings, or the farms of the settlement.
This was called chain gang guard duty, because the
prisoners for most part worked in chains shackled
together.   Truly it was a sad and heartrending
spectacle, for, although these men were nearly all
double-dyed villains and ruffians of the worst class,
yet one could not but feel some degree of pity for
their awful lot, and the everlasting clank, clank of
their chains amid the beauties of Nature about us
and them seemed to me a very strange and terrible
contrast.

Under Lieutenant King the settlement had made great progress. He had erected many good and substantial buildings and made excellent roads about the island, and had some fine crops growing on the place. But all this had not been effected with the lazy rascals who were supposed to do the work without much wholesome punishment, and the convicts for the most part had had the impudence all taken out of them by a free use of the triangles when we landed on the island. For although Lieutenant King was naturally a fair man, he was a better officer.

The attempt to grow flax had, however, been a failure, though it was expected, as time went on, the settlers would by experience succeed in their efforts, and profit by the skill of Mr Morley, the gentleman adventurer of whom I have spoken, and who had accompanied Lieutenant King to teach the prisoners how to manufacture the raw material. Indeed, long after this, one of the following Governors at Port Jackson thought much of raising flax on the island, and a ship was sent to New Zealand from Port Jackson to capture some of the native Mowrees, as the savages of that country are called, and bring them to Norfolk Island, for they are well skilled in its cultivation, and Captain Cook had seen them manufacture it into a rude cloth.

The island reminded me very much of my old home. It is a beautiful, fertile spot, all hills and dales, and bright green grass, and was very like the Isle of Wight, but not so large.

However, we were all too miserable and anxious to be relieved to think much of these things then, I can tell you, and very joyous we were when at the end of the eleven months the *Supply* hove in sight off Sydney Bay, and we lucky ones of the detachment who belonged to the ship's company of the *Sirius* marched down to the shore with drums beating and light hearts, and tumbled into the boats to take up our quarters on board the brig, which was taking us back to Port Jackson.

CHAPTER XXII

THE SECOND FLEET ARRIVES AND WE HEAR NEWS FROM HOME

The gallant little *Supply* landed us in Port Jackson on the twenty-sixth of February, 1791, and as soon as we had disembarked we heard that many important events had happened during our absence.

When we left the settlement for Norfork Island, the Governor had wisely put every person on short rations, but when the news came of the disaster to the *Sirius*, they were still further reduced, and then the prisoners became too weak to work very much. The rations served out were only two pounds and a half of floor, two pounds of pork, and two pounds of rice, to seven persons for one day.

So the *Supply* was sent to Batavia, under Lieutenant Ball, for all the provisions she could carry, with orders to get back as quickly as possible, and the poor, hungry folks on shore watched her sail away with very depressed hearts, knowing it would be long, weary months ere she returned. And, indeed,

it was nearly six months ere she came back, but
sad to say, she brought back but eight months'
supplies for her own people, for provisions were
scarce at Batavia; but Lieutenant Ball gladdened
the hearts of the people by informing Captain Phillip
that he had chartered the Dutch snow *Waaksamheyd* to follow him with a cargo of stores. The
Dutchman, however, did not arrive till December,
and in the meantime the *Lady Juliana* had arrived
from England, so the Dutch skipper, whose name
was Smith, was not so welcome as he would have
been had he arrived a little earlier.

The *Lady Juliana* was the first ship to arrive in
Port Jackson of the second fleet of convicts sent to
the colony. This second fleet consisted of the
Justinian store ship, the *Surprize*, *Neptune*, *Scarboro*,
and the *Lady Juliana* convict transports, carrying
between them nearly one thousand three hundred
prisoners, and the *Guardian* man-o'-war, converted
into a store ship, and which was injured by an ice-
berg and beached at Table Bay. The fleet left
England in the middle of the year 1789, and the
Lady Juliana brought letters and despatches up to
July twenty-eighth of that year. When she was
sighted at the look-out point on June the third,
1790, the flag was run up signalling that a ship was
in sight.

A very exciting scene followed this news, many
of the people actually weeping for joy. As she was

working in between the heads, the Governor put off
to her, but his return damped the joy of the unhappy
people when it was known that she had brought
with her over two hundred female prisoners, and
only a few provisions saved from the *Guardian*.

She brought exciting news. A bloody revolution
was going on in France, and our own King, George
the Third, had been so ill that a Regency was
appointed to govern the kingdom, but our people
at the settlement rejoiced that he was now quite
recovered.

She brought letters for many of the poor exiles,
and Lieutenant Fairfax heard of the death of the
old squire, his father. Miss Charlotte Fairfax wrote
this letter, and the lieutenant was so good as to
read portions of it to me when he saw me on my
return from Norfolk Island, and his sister had actually
remembered me, for she wrote : — 'Tell the lad
Dew, who sailed for Botany Bay with you, that his
father's health is breaking and that he grows anxious
for his return.' Then in another part of the letter
Miss Fairfax urged the lieutenant to come home as
soon as possible and bring me with him, that I might
comfort my father in his old age. Indeed, her kind
words concerning so humble a person as myself
brought the water to my eyes, and affected me quite
as much as did the sad news about my poor father's
health.

The wreck of the *Guardian* was a serious disaster

to us, for she was a fast ship, and had a fine lot of
stores for the settlement, and by her loss we were
left with a great increase to our population, but
with no sensible addition to our means of feeding
them. Fortunately, seventeen days later, the *Justinian*
arrived laden entirely with stores, and within eight
days the *Surprize*, the *Scarboro* and the *Neptune* had
all made the port. The fleet had had a terrible
voyage, for on the three last-named ships alone
two hundred and sixty-seven persons had perished
out of one thousand and six who sailed, and three
weeks after the ships arrived, fifty more had died
and four hundred and fifty were on the sick list,
the remainder being too ill to attend to themselves.
The voyage had been full of mutinies, and dreadful bloodshed and troubles of all sorts; and everyone
of the officers on board, so my comrades told me,
looked worn out with the terrible days of ceaseless
anxiety they had gone through. The sight the
prisoners presented when they were landed, many
of them still heavily ironed, was a very horrid one,
and the filthy condition of some of the most dangerous
of them was revolting to the eye of every decent
person.

There was a great fuss made about this voyage
in England afterwards; but all this is another story,
and I must come back to what concerns me alone.

The guards on these ships were furnished by men
from a new regiment called the New South Wales

Corps (the 102d Regiment), which was raised for service in the settlement. The remainder of this regiment was coming out in a third fleet of transports, and on board of His Majesty's ship *Gorgon*, which was to take the Marines home to England. Our battalion was told that the men might re-enlist for service in the colony in the new regiment ; but you may depend very few of our men volunteered, and there was much rejoicing and looking forward to the arrival of the *Gorgon* to take us home. Indeed, I think the sight of the landing of the people from the second fleet proved too much for many of our men, and made them eager to be away from such horrors.

CHAPTER XXIII

THE LIEUTENANT AND MYSELF MEET WITH A
GREAT DISAPPOINTMENT, AND I MAKE THE
ACQUAINTANCE OF THE DUTCH CAPTAIN OF
THE *WAAKSAMHEYD*

ACCORDING to the dispatches that Captain Phillip
had received from England, the *Gorgon* ought to
have arrived long before we returned from Norfolk
Island in the *Supply*, and as month after month
went by, and there was no sign of her, the governor
determined to send the ship's company of the *Sirius*
home in the Dutch snow,* the *Waaksamheyd*, which
was taken into the service as a transport, and we
were greatly rejoiced at the prospect of a speedy
return. Already the men of the new regiment
and the Marines were at loggerheads, and we
had fights occurring very frequently; the new men
were certainly, to my mind, a very indifferent and
badly-disciplined regiment when compared to my
corps.

In those times much of the discipline of the

---

* A snow was a vessel with fore and main masts, and with another
short mast stepped very far aft.

service was relaxed, and so it was that Lieutenant
Fairfax, who was now a much older and graver-
looking man, would get talking to me, when I was
off duty, quite familiarly.

The Bryants, he one day told me, were doing
very well now. A second child had been born to
them, and I thought it no little presumption on
their part, and very good-natured of Mr Fairfax not
to be offended, that they had named the child
Charlotte, after Mary's former mistress, Miss
Fairfax of Solcombe Manor House. Will Bryant
had now charge of the settlement fishing station,
and, with his crew, was employed in fishing about
the numerous bays in Port Jackson, he being
allowed to cruise in any part of the bay inside
the heads.

Only a few days after the lieutenant had told
us about the chartering of the *Waaksamheyd*, he
came to me with a very long face.

'Sergeant, this is indeed hard lines; we are not
going home after all until the *Gorgon* arrives.
Only the actual ship's company of the *Sirius* go
home in the snow.'

'How then, sir,' said I, 'do we not belong to
the *Sirius?*'

'The Governor has had my name taken off her
books ever since she left for the Cape of Good
Hope, and I have to do guard duty here until
relieved by the remainder of the new regiment.

And as you belong to my company, Dew, you, too, will have to remain. The Governor said he was very sorry for us both, but duty, you know, sergeant.'

This was sad news for me, and as the lieutenant walked moodily away I thought of my poor old father, and wondered if I should see him again ; but it was worse for Mr Fairfax, whose estates badly wanted a man's management to put and keep them in order.

And so it came about that our brave Captain Hunter and the sailors of the *Sirius* went home in the Dutch snow, and had a dreadful voyage, meeting with bad weather and much sickness. They sailed out of Port Jackson on the morning of March the twenty-seventh, 1791, and arrived at Portsmouth on April the twenty-second, 1792. There Captain Hunter was tried by court-martial for the loss of the *Sirius*, and was honourably acquitted.

But before the Dutchman left Port Jackson on this voyage, there occurred a very momentous event in the history of Mary and Will Bryant, and the master of the *Waaksamheyd* was greatly concerned therein, as you will see later on.

His ship lay at her anchor off the Farm Cove, after she had discharged her stores, and a gang of men were working on board, putting in some fittings in her 'tween decks, to receive the men

from the *Sirius*. The captain of the snow was a
Dutchman, whose proper name, I have no doubt,
was Schmidt, but who always wrote it Smith,
I suppose, because he had the honour to sail under
English colours since the Governor had chartered him.

He was a big, fat, greasy-looking fellow, with
the look of a brewer's storeman disguised in a cloak
and Guy Fawkes hat, like all the Dutchmen I
had ever seen at Portsmouth looked. I got to
know him very well by sight before he sailed; he
was such a coarse, gross-looking man that I could
not help disliking him even then.

At this time I had just been put in charge of
the Farm Cove guard-room, which was situated
some little distance from the water's edge, but
right on the road to the Governor's house, and
not far from the huts of the fishing settlement;
and every time this great Dutch seal came waddl-
ing ashore, he had, in order to reach the main
settlement, to first pass the fishing huts of Will
Bryant and his party, and then the main guard-
room; and as he always came ashore every day,
he soon became quite a familiar person to us all.

Now, as soon as I was appointed to my new post,
I knew that what I had dreaded from the first day
of my arrival at the settlement had come to pass,
and it had become my duty to act as gaoler over
poor Will Bryant and the woman whose love I had
once sought.

A list of the prisoners in this fishing village was furnished to me, and I was glad to read that I was not in any way to interfere with them so long as they behaved themselves.

As I have already said, Will Bryant was, by reason of his good conduct, placed in charge of the gang, whose names I will here set down on account of the adventure in which they afterwards took part.

First, then, there was Will Bryant and Mary his wife, and the children Emanuel and Charlotte. He was described in my list as of first-class behaviour, and the family, so my orders ran, having proved by their good conduct that they were entitled to every consideration consistent with the penal discipline of the settlement, were to be interfered with as little as possible. Then there were James Martin, James Cox and Samuel Bird *alias* John Simms, all of whom had landed with us in the first fleet, and who were all 'good conduct' men ; William Allen, John Butcher, Nathaniel Lilley and William Morton, who had been landed from the second fleet, and knowing something of boats, had been sent to Farm Cove to work in Bryant's gang.

The guard was made up of myself, a corporal and four privates, and from these, sentries were found to guard the Government buildings, which now stretched from our guard-house across to Sydney Cove. But one sentry was on duty at night-time, posted outside the guard-room to give the alarm in case of sudden outbreak, the only danger we feared. Our guard-house was situated about half a mile from the shore, where the boats were hauled up on the mud and made fast by chains to posts. These chains were secured by a pair of handcuffs, and it was the duty of the corporal of the guard to see them locked and then hang the keys up in the guard-room.

During the day-time Bryant was responsible for the boats, and it was none of my business to interfere with him so long as his gang did not idle their time away, and kept good order.

Bryant was the only married man in the party, and he lived with his wife and two children in a hut some little distance from that occupied by the other men.

I took charge of this post on the twenty-fourth of March, 1791, at noon, and as soon as the relieved guard marched off and I had seen my sentries properly posted, I walked down to the shore to see the Bryants.

Will was busy, with the help of two of his men, in putting a new plank in the big boat, and the rest of the gang were away fishing in the harbour, or mending their nets some distance from us.

Mary sat at the door of the hut nursing her infant, and her other child, a fine, sturdy little fellow with fair, curly hair and blue eyes like his father, played at her feet. I only caught one glance at her face, which seemed to me to be thin and worn, but yet her dark eyes had all their old beauty in them.

'I am glad to see that your good conduct has led
to your being given this job, Will Bryant,' said I ;
'keep going straight and I'll not interfere with you.'

'Oh, you are the new sergeant of the guard, sir,'
replied my old acquaintance. 'I thank you for your
kindness and will try to keep straight, as you say.'
I thought that remark of mine would serve the
purpose of hinting to Will that a man in my position could not make his duty fit in with any intimacy
with him or his wife, and Will's answer showed, as
he stood to attention when he gave it, that he quite
understood my meaning.

'That is your wife over there, I think,' I went
on, as if Mary was a stranger to me, and nodding
towards the hut. Will was as quick to see my
meaning, and understood that I thought it best his
fellow-prisoners should not know of our former
intimacy.

'Yes, sir, that is my wife and children,' he
answered.

'Very good. You may tell her from me tha
while you go on as you have been doing all will
be well with you,' and with this I wheeled about
and marched off, never once looking towards Mary,
or giving her an opportunity of speaking to me.

CHAPTER XXIV

As I have said, this fat Dutchman, Captain Detmar Smith, of the *Waaksamheyd*, came on shore every day, and I noticed that he always stopped at the fishing settlement on his way to the Government buildings, where he transacted his business.

On the second day after I had been placed at my new post I saw that he had struck up an acquaintance with the Bryants, and on nearly every other day since I had seen him talking and laughing with Mary. He always, after stepping out of his boat, made his way to the fishing settlement, and waddled up to the Bryants' hut, where he was in full view from the guard-house.

It would have been my duty to put a stop to this if the Bryants had been like ordinary prisoners, but Will was now a kind of constable over his gang, and as I had been expressly ordered by my superiors, and by Lieutenant Fairfax in particular, not to

175

harass him in any way, I could not see my way to interfere.

When the transports were lying at anchor in the Cove, it was the custom to put a sentry on board of them to keep the prisoners from stowing away or stealing the ships' boats, but I had no orders to do this with the Dutch snow, because it was well understood that no prisoners were likely to stow themselves on board of her as she was to take home the crew of a King's ship. As to stealing her boats, Bryant had already two boats of which he might be said to have full charge, and no suspicion of his loyalty ever occurred to my superiors, so that the only matter I had to look to in connection with the eleven souls who made up the little settlement, was to see that Bryant and his seven men were in their quarters at sunset. As to Mary and her two children, of course I had no right to concern myself.

But, for all the trust put in Bryant's loyalty, I thought it my duty to keep my eyes open so far as his gang was concerned. I had no fear of the man himself, with his wife and two infants. I was sure he was safe enough ; but his men might, I thought, at any moment take it into their heads to make a dash for their liberty.

Prisoners were very foolish in this matter, and although 'twas almost certain death to them, they often ran away into the woods and were never more heard of, dying, no doubt, by the hands of the savages or by starvation. So foolish were they that a large party once went away thinking they might reach China by constantly walking north, while in September, 1790, five men stole a punt from near Rose Hill and sailed her outside of the heads, never more being heard of; and, no doubt, they soon went to the bottom.

And so, when I noticed this big, greasy Dutchman and the Bryants getting friendly, I wondered very much what it meant, although I could in no way at first connect this circumstance with any attempt at escaping.

One day I thought I would see if anything was to be got out of Smith, and so as he was passing the guard-house and nodding a good-day to me, I stopped him and said,—

' Good-day, Mr Smith, I notice that you seem to take an interest in the Bryants. Of course, you know, it is against the regulations to have any dealings with prisoners.'

He turned short round when I said this, and stepped up close to me, and putting a fat, dirty finger in a buttonhole of my tunic, rocked me to and fro by the sheer weight of his flabby arm. He spoke English but poorly, and he seemed to jerk the words out in a fat, wheezy voice as if his inside were lined with wool.

' Shoost look here, mein freindt, dake my advites

M

und do not inderferes mit a man's loaf affairdts.
Der vrow of dis Bryandts is a very nice womans,
und I do lide to dork mit her ; und so, meinheer,
do you not trooble, but make some moneys by mind
you business.'

I could have struck the big, fat, oily fool as he
leered at me with his dead, fish-like eyes, but I
thought better of it, for I guessed he was not the
kind of man that a high-spirited woman like Mary
Bryant would fall in love with, and that, whatever
of love-making there was, was all on his side. So I
only answered, 'Very good, Mr Smith ; but, remember my duty is to see the regulations carried
out, and so there must be no trading or inter-
ference with these people. Speak to them in a
friendly way as much as you like, but don't make
too sure that Mistress Bryant is in love with you.'

'Yah, I onderstood der reguladions and I dakes
care nod to break dem. Got-day, young soldier
mans,' and then he waddled off to the Government
buildings.

On that same evening I saw the fellow meet
Mary Bryant some distance from her hut, when
her husband was on the shore making fast his boat,
and I saw him hand her a big canvas sailor's bag,
so heavy that, though she was no weakly woman,
she could scarcely drag it to the door of the hut,
where I watched her later on leave it.

But worse than this, the fellow held her hand in

his, and sure enough, from where I watched, I could see plainly enough that she was lending a willing ear to his love-making.

Now this vexed me mightily. Clearly it was my duty to interfere, for this great, greasy Dutchman had no right to be giving bags of stores to prisoners, and if Mary Bryant, by association with vicious and wicked persons had come to this, I must not allow my charges to be thus corrupted.

Mr Fairfax was the officer of the guard for the next day, and when in the morning he visited the guard-room, I called him aside and told him all about it.

'Sergeant,' said he, wheeling round, and looking me square in the face, 'have you ever known me to neglect my duty?'

'Sir,' I answered respectfully, 'do you suppose I would dare to think of such a thing?'

'Very well, then. Let me give you a piece of advice. You are the youngest sergeant in this detachment, and, in consequence, you are apt to be a little over-zealous. You see things that you ought not see, and —and in point of fact, Dew, you are a devilish good fellow in your way, but, for goodness' sake, don't be so confoundedly fussy. I remember a certain little matter before we left Portsmouth, in which you committed a breach of the regulations and helped an old rascal to smuggle a cask of French brandy. Now, if I—eh?'

I hung my head at this and muttered, 'True, sir, you were very good-natured to me and I was very foolish.'

'Quite so; but remember, Dew, these poor Bryants, by a little flirtation on the part of Mary with this fat Dutchman, have probably managed to get a bag of flour for the youngsters, or something of that kind, and if you don't see, why, there's no harm done. God knows the little children may need a change of food.'

Then I saluted and he walked away; but all the same, the more I thought of it the more determined I was to have a word or two with Mary on the subject, and so I watched an opportunity, and the next afternoon, which was the twenty-eighth, just before the boats came in I walked over to the hut and called her out to speak to me.

'What do you want with me, Sergeant Dew?' she asked in her old, quick way.

'Mrs Bryant,' said I, ''tis a matter of duty that brings me here. I have seen your goings on with the master of the Dutch snow, and I warn you that you must not—'

'What have you seen?' and she turned upon me with a dangerous flash in her dark eyes.

'I have seen him give you a bag full of flour or something of the sort, and I have seen him making love to you and you encouraging him.'

'Listen to me, Will, and forgive me for calling you by the old name, you who are now so much above the

likes of me ; I have as much dislike to that Dutchman
as 'tis possible for woman to have, but,' and there
came a sad sobbing break in her voice that went
straight to my heart, 'my two poor infants are half-
starved and crave for more food.   Will, Will, forget
for once that you are a sergeant, forget for once that
you are our gaoler, forget for once that Will and I are
marked by the hand of felony, innocent though we
are ; but remember, and surely you will remember,
Will, what I once was when you knew me in the
days gone by for ever.'

Now, man as I was, the woman's pleading voice
shook me strangely and as she stood there with her
hands clasped together, as she had clasped them the
day she had met Lieutenant Fairfax on the ship's
deck at the Cape of Good Hope, I had to turn my
face away.

She stood thus for a minute or so, and her bosom
heaved quickly under her poor, shabby gown, and her
great, black eyes, soft enough now, filled with tears,
and then she spoke again, her voice full of quavering
prayer.

'For the sake of the old days, Will ; for the sake
of my innocent, suffering children who are as dear to
the sight of God, born as they are in a felon's land,
as if they had been born in England ; for theirs, and
mine and Will's sakes, do not take away from us that
which the foreign captain has given us.   And, Will,
if I did by a little harmless trickery take this bag

from him, it was because, as the Almighty is my witness, that which was in it will prove our salvation. So I pray you do not judge me too harshly.'

'Heaven forgive me, Mary, if I did so, but you know that I must do my duty, and besides, what would your husband say if he saw you holding that fat fool's hand, as I did?'

'Dear Sergeant Dew, my poor Will is too loyal and true to the Governor—Heaven bless him! for he is a good man—not to be very angry with me if he had a thought that I took aught from the Dutchman, so say no more about it, and I promise you I will never speak to the Dutchman again as long as the ship is here;' and she dried her tears and smiled into my face.

'On that condition, Mary, there's an end of the matter, and I am glad your husband knows nothing of it,' and I turned to walk away.

'Good-bye, sergeant; won't you shake hands for the sake of the old times.'

'Good-bye,' said I, 'and certainly I will shake hands, but we shall often see each other, I daresay, though I don't think it well to appear friendly with you, because, duty, you know, forbids.'

Then I shook hands with her, and went back to my quarters, feeling that Mary Bryant was at any-rate an honest woman, and safe from temptation by reason of the love she bore her children.

CHAPTER XXV

A STILL GREATER AND VERY DARING BREACH OF THE REGULATIONS IS COMMITTED BY WILL BRYANT AND HIS GANG

The news of the wonderful voyage made by Lieutenant Bligh in an open boat after he had been set adrift with some good men by his mutinous mate, Fletcher Christian, had reached our settlement by the ships of the second fleet, and I often pondered over it and thought it would be nothing to marvel at if some of our prisoners tried something of this nature. But I had no fear of Bryant. Happily married and with two infant children, there was little fear that he would dare upon such a hazardous venture, though I did sometimes fear that some of his crew might steal a boat and make the attempt. It was with some thought of this in my mind that, when I returned to the guard-house on the evening of my talk with Mary Bryant, which was the twenty-eighth of March, 1791, I took particular notice that the keys of the locks on the boat moorings were hanging in the guard-room at ten o'clock, when I turned in for the night.

I felt pretty easy in my mind, because our fishing boats were very poor. The big boat was in use with the fishing gang at Botany Bay, and the two boats in Bryant's charge were much too small for venturing outside the heads in. One of them was a small ship's gig; the other was rather larger, pulled six oars, and was rigged cutter fashion. She had just been repaired by the fishermen and was in good order, but I thought it would be little short of madness, though the weather was at this season fine, to venture to sea in her.

The next morning at daybreak I was awakened by the cry of the sentry, 'Guard, turn out.' Every man of us ran to the door, seizing our muskets on the way, and wondering what had happened.

'What is it, sentry?' said I, seeing nothing to call us for in the dim morning light.

'The boat, sergeant,' said he; 'the biggest boat is gone.'

Sure enough she was gone.

'Broken away from her moorings and drifted to sea,' said the corporal.

'Don't be a fool,' said I. 'How could she get off the mud and break her chain? Fall in, and let us see how many prisoners are left, for that's what's the matter. Bryant's hut first; he may be able to help us.'

And so we marched across to Bryant's hut, and knocked loudly at the door, but to my great fear got

no answer to our knocking.   Then without ceremony
we opened the door and walked in, and the next
moment I understood all that had happened.

There was no one in the place, and the clothes
which usually hung on its walls were missing.   The
hut floor was boarded, and one of the boards had been
taken up, and was lying beside a hole scooped in the
earth, that 'twas plain had been used to conceal something in.

It was no use standing about looking at this, so I
marched my men to the hut in which the unmarried
prisoners were quartered, and found that the whole
seven of them were gone.   But, placed in one of the
men's bunks where it could not be easily seen unless
strict search was made for it, was a big sheet of paper
folded and addressed to Sarah Young.   This woman
was, I knew, a female prisoner that James Cox, one of
Bryant's gang, was waiting for permission to marry,
and so I seized the letter and made no scruple of
reading it.   This is what it said,—

'DEAR SARAH,—Do you give over those vices that I have caught you at
more than once, or you will come to a bad end.   If you had been a different woman I should not have joined these mad men, or I would have
taken you with me.   We hope to reach Timor.   We have a compass
and a quadrant which Will Bryant got from you know who, and there
are those among us who know how to use them.   Good-bye.—Your
friend,   'JAMES COX.'

After reading this, I traced the footmarks of the
fugitives down to the boat's mooring post, where I

found the chain was filed through, and scattered
about were some four or five pounds of rice, which the
fugitives had spilled in their hurry. The big seine
was lying in its place, but one that Bryant had been
making for use in the small boat, and which was
a very handy net, was missing, and I now remembered
that I had wondered why he had taken so long over
the job.

The next thing to do was to report the matter, and
so I sent a man post-haste to headquarters, and soon
Lieutenant Fairfax came to the guard-house.

As soon as he saw me he beckoned me over to him,
and said hurriedly, in a low tone,—

'You remember our talk the other day? Well,
what you said was quite right, and I was wrong.
For Heaven's sake be quiet about it. I am in no
good odour with my superiors now, and there will
be the devil to pay, and no pitch hot, if my careless-
ness comes to light.'

'Have no fear, sir,' says I, 'for you'll find that you
can trust me, sir. I have been in a scrape myself.'

I couldn't help reminding him that once he had
obliged me by holding his tongue, and now I was to
oblige him, though 'twas mighty disrespectful.

'Good man, Dew,' he answered, 'and when we get
out of this infernal settlement I'll settle down and lead
a quiet country life with no regulations to break, and
I'll buy you out, and you shall be my tenant as your
father was my father's.'

Then he said, so that the others could hear him,
-'I am afraid we will never catch them, because
we have no boat to chase them with, and the chances
are, by the time we get the big boat round from Botany
Bay, they will be all at the bottom, or eaten by the
sharks.'

CHAPTER XXVI

I AM HOMEWARD BOUND

THE news of the escape of the Bryants spread like wildfire among the people of the settlement, and many of the prisoners showed their excitement very plainly. At twelve o'clock Lieutenant Fairfax and myself were brought before the Governor to give our version of the matter.

His Excellency was greatly put about, but he could scarcely blame me or my men, although he wanted to know how it was the fugitives had got hold of stores and water without the guard knowing anything about it; and he also wanted to know who was the man referred to in James Cox's letter to the woman Young.

I said I could not tell, but that I suspected.

'Who do you suspect?' asked the Governor.

'Mr Smith, the master of the Dutch snow,' I answered.

'Why do you think he helped them?'

Before I could answer, the lieutenant broke in. Said he,—

'As a matter of fact, sir, Sergeant Dew reported

to me that this man was seen talking a good deal
to the Bryants, and I told him not to interfere ;
they were not to be molested while they behaved
themselves.'

'Oh, indeed,' said the Governor, 'that will do.
Sergeant Dew, I don't think you or your men are
to blame ; you may go.'

Then afterwards I heard that the Governor gave
the lieutenant a great talking to for taking things
so easy, and by the way, said he,—

'These are the persons you took so much interest
in on the voyage out, are they not, lieutenant?'

'Yes, sir, but I hope you don't think I relaxed
my duty on that account.'

'We will say no more about it, Mr Fairfax,'
said Captain Phillip, rising from his seat. 'You will
be leaving the settlement shortly, and no good can
come of any fuss that is made now, and so I have
nothing more to say.'

And, so far, the matter ended ; but my lieutenant
told me, a few evenings afterwards, the Governor sent
for him again and, producing a chart, showed Mr
Fairfax the course that these wretched people would
most likely take, and although the Governor spoke
very angrily of Bryant and the other men, he said
to the lieutenant that, for the sake of the poor
woman and the tender children, he would be pleased
to hear that they had been picked up by some ship, or
had reached some haven of safety on the coast. That

they could ever reach the East Indies was, of course, quite out of the question ; and then the two fell to talking of the strange and wonderful voyage of Lieutenant Bligh, who had navigated his boat four thousand miles from Otaheite to Cowpang without losing a man. Captain Phillip, it appeared, thought that the fugitives would soon see the folly of their attempting a similar voyage in such a wretched cockershell, and would run ashore somewhere on the coast near Port Jackson, and live hiding in the woods.

The time now began to hang heavily upon our hands waiting for the *Gorgon* to take us home, and she was so long on the passage, that we really began to entertain fears for her safety.

Up to the time of her arrival, which was on the twenty-first of September, nothing of great moment happened that I need record here, except that the natives were occasionally very troublesome, and the Governor tried all in his power to make friends with them, even going the length of capturing one or two of them, and trying to teach them civilised manners and customs.

The Marines, both officers and men, were offered a choice of becoming settlers in the country, and some of them were also asked to join the New South Wales Regiment. Mr Fairfax would not think of this for a moment, and I was quite of his opinion, and was glad enough, I can tell you, to embark on the *Gorgon*, which we did on the tenth day of

December 1791, and sailed away from Port Jackson on our voyage to England.

The third fleet had arrived in the previous month, bringing 1695 male and 168 female prisoners and another detachment of the new regiment, and we got away just in time to escape further suffering from short provisions.

My old commandant, Major Ross, and the headquarters company of our detachment, was also able to leave in the *Gorgon*, by the arrival of the transports bringing more troops.

And now I have told you all that concerned my stay in the settlement at Port Jackson, which all the folks on this side of the world will still insist upon calling Botany Bay.

You will learn, from what I have written, that although I had served over four years in the service, and had never seen a shot fired at the enemy, for the miserable savages, and almost as unhappy prisoners, could scarcely be counted as the King's enemies, yet I had risen to the rank of sergeant by a steady attention to my duty, and perhaps deserved my three stripes quite as much as men who had been engaged in shooting down their fellow-creatures amid the stirring scenes of war that the ballad-mongers sing of.

CHAPTER XXVII

I MEET WITH A GREAT SURPRISE AT THE CAPE
OF GOOD HOPE, AND LIEUTENANT FAIRFAX
LOSES HIS DIGNITY

THE *Gorgon* sailed out of Sydney Cove with a very
strong, hot wind from the westward, and we soon
settled down cheerfully enough to life on board the
ship, for we knew that every day brought us nearer
home. The ship was a very good sailer, and there
was a vast difference between her and the old *Sirius*.
On the *Sirius* every seaman swore at being sent to
sea in such a tub, as they called her ; but the sailors
of the *Gorgon* were very proud of their ship, and
certainly she was a very comfortable and fast craft.

Nothing of moment happened until we reached
the Cape of Good Hope, but on the passage, Mr
Fairfax, who, now that we were so soon to return
to civilian life, grew every day more condescending
towards me, and often talked with me over our
strange adventures.

He had fully made up his mind to leave the
Service when we got to England, and for my own
part I was glad and thankful for the promise he had
made me, that he would help to purchase my dis-

charge as soon as he could come at his estate and set his affairs in order.

We more than once spoke of the foolhardy venture of the Bryants, never doubting that they had perished miserably, for what could eleven persons, two of them tender children and one a woman, ever hope to do towards reaching civilisation in such a frail craft as was their open boat.

I remember that one night when we were speaking of this matter, one of the ship's officers joined us and told us that among his other adventures he had been cast away in a country ship in the East Indies, and that he and the master and seven or eight of the crew had voyaged 700 miles in an open boat to the island of Ceylon, and that, though their boat had twice capsized, yet none of them lost their lives, although they suffered the very greatest agonies from thirst. His story made me remark to my lieutenant that perhaps, after all, the Bryants might have gone a great distance before disaster overtook them ; but the *Gorgon* officer said it would not be possible for such a small and overcrowded boat as we had described, to live out even a moderate gale. And so the very faint hope that I had begun to cherish about Will and Mary died away altogether ; for this officer was a very able and good officer, and had been forty-two years in King's ships.

We arrived at the Cape of Good Hope in March, 1792, and soon completed taking in our stores, and were

N

within twenty-four hours of getting under weigh, when a Dutch vessel entered the bay, and as soon as she saw our ensign, hoisted the private signal, and a boat was sent to her.

When the officer in charge returned, he brought with him the news that the Dutchman was a vessel chartered at Batavia by Captain Edwards of the *Pandora*, a King's ship.

The *Pandora* had been sent to Otaheite to search for the mutineers of the *Bounty*. She had secured some of them, and was proceeding on her way home, when she was wrecked, on August twenty-eighth, 1791, on a coral reef off the north coast of New Holland. Eighty-nine of the *Pandora's* crew and ten out of the fourteen mutineers were saved, and after a terrible boat voyage made their way to Timor, where they had arrived on September the fifteenth, 1791.

It now fell out that we were to convey these persons to England, and all our boats were got out to bring them on board.

When the boats ranged alongside with these poor people on board, I leant over the rail watching them, and thinking of the unfortunate Bryants. If Captain Bligh, whose sufferings I had heard of, had had such a terrible experience in his boat voyage; if Captain Edwards and his crew had suffered greater hardships than it is possible to describe in their journey in their boats, what chance had these poor, ignorant creatures—one of them a woman with two tender infants—what chance had these of surviving such an undertaking ?

It was with such thoughts that my mind was occupied, when Mr Fairfax tapped me on the shoulder and asked me of what I was thinking, and I told him.

I noticed that as he spoke to me he was strangely moved, and that his face flushed and then paled again, as if he were seized with a vertigo or fever, and before I had got out my answer to his question, he interrupted me, and gripped my arm very tightly.

'Dew, my lad; you do not know all. For God's sake, man, look over the side at that boat now coming alongside, and see if you can recognise her.'

He almost dragged me further along the deck, to where we could get a better view of those who were in the boat, and looking down, I saw, but could scarce recognise, the face of the woman who, but a few moments before, had been in my thoughts.

A Marine who stood on the foot of the landing-stage held out his hand to help her out of the boat, then I saw that the sadly-altered, wasted and feeble creature who stood up with trembling feet to step upon the *Gorgon's* ladder, was indeed Mary Bryant. With one hand she held, clasped to her breast, the little infant, the namesake of her former mistress.

With slow and laboured steps she toiled up to

the gangway, assisted by the Marine, and when in a dazed, melancholy way her great, dark eyes, so full of suffering and pain, for a moment rested upon the ship's company, I felt a quick gush of tears come to mine, and turned away my head.

'God help the poor wench; 'tis cruel hard,' said an old boatswain's mate beside me; and, indeed, from all sides there came a murmuring sympathy for the poor girl.

But Mr Fairfax, forgetting rank, and station, and all else, rushed to the gangway, and pushing aside the rough but honest hands of those who sought to help her, took Mary in his arms, child and all, and carried her to a hatchway; then, before she could realise this act of my patron's, and who it was whose heart was so big and noble as to have naught else for her but tender pity, she fainted dead away; and then all the rough men who stood about her strove who should be the first to help the surgeon and Mr Fairfax in his endeavours to restore her to life, and not a man among us all, but respected the lieutenant for that generous act of his, or spoke of it afterwards but as proof of his noble manliness. Indeed, the old boatswain's mate, who had spoken so pityingly to me about Mary, turned to those about him, and, with a very dreadful oath, for which, I am sure, he was pardoned by the Power above, said that the

soldier officer was a good sailor spoiled, and ought
to be an Admiral.

I had no eyes nor thought of others but of
Mary at this time, and stood like a fool, just
stupidly looking on, as they chafed her hands and
tried to restore the little life remaining in her.
But when I had recovered my senses a little, I
learned that all that remained of the poor creatures
who had escaped from the settlement were come
on board; and here I will set down who they
were.   First, there was Mary and the infant
Charlotte, and then James Martin, John Butcher,
William Allan and Nathaniel Lilley.   These six
were all the survivors of the eleven souls who had
left Port Jackson a whole year before.

Mary, when she had recovered a little, was
tenderly carried below, and Captain Parker of the
Gorgon, good-hearted man, ordered that she should
be well tended by the ship's surgeon, and placed in
one of the officer's cabins at the after end of
the ship, which was readily given up to her.

No words of mine can describe the alteration
that I saw in her, and even the four strong men
were so different, and had grown so old and worn
with hardships, that I scarcely knew them again,
and their dreadful appearance, felons though they
were, filled me with the strongest pity.

And so, in a few hours after this, we were once
more under weigh, bound for England, and down

below, on the lower deck, lay the poor prisoners.
Alas! I thought, what will our arrival in England
mean to them?

But Mr Fairfax bestirred himself, and so did everyone on board, to do the best that could be done for
these unhappy creatures, and as the days at sea
went by, bit by bit he got from Mary a history
of the terrible adventure she had passed through,
and it was all written out, to present as a Petition
to the authorities for her forgiveness. And so the
history of this ever-memorable voyage was set
down in full by my lieutenant, in Mary's own
words, as nearly as could be done, save where the
prisoner Butcher, whom he afterwards saw very
often in Newgate, supplied particulars of the
places they had touched at, and some other
matters of which poor Mary had no knowledge;
and in this form I here relate it; and in no book
or printed paper whatsoever has this complete and
truthful account ever before been set down; therefore, preserve it, so that your children and their
children may read the particulars of this memorable
voyage. And I trust that God in His mercy, should
any of you adventure in foreign lands, may preserve
you from such awful dangers that befell Mary and
her unhappy companions in misery.

CHAPTER XXVIII

MARY BEGINS HER STORY

IT was I, and I alone, who brought this dreadful suffering upon us; and I pray that He who knows our weak human nature will forgive and pardon me for sacrificing, by my mad and insensate folly, the lives of those unhappy men and my innocent child.

My husband had grown contented with our lot, and by his good and steady conduct and industry had won not only the confidence and good opinion of Captain Phillip, but that of all the officers of the settlement.

Though 'tis nearly five weary years ago since the day that he and I, with our vile and hardened companions, were landed on the shores of Port Jackson, and we met for the first time after long months of severance, yet as long as God gives me life I shall never forget the soft, tender light in his brave, blue eyes when he sprang to my side and, amid the jeers and foul and mocking jests of the abandoned felons who surrounded us, took my hands in his and pressed his lips to mine.

'Mary, Mary, my own brave girl,' he said, and I felt his great, strong chest beat and throb as he pressed me to his heart, 'may God help me to be a good husband to you.' And then soon after came our marriage, so strange a marriage as it was. Not as I had once thought of it, when Will had first told me he loved me as we sat in a little nook on Solcombe Cliffs two years before; for he had promised me that after he had run but one cargo more he would give up smuggling, and then come to the Manor House and claim me for his wife. 'And, Mary,' said he, 'because you have stuck to me and believed in me when the old women have croaked and sought to make mischief between us, I will show them such a wedding when we are married that it won't easily be forgotten by Solcombe folks, or, indeed, anywhere on the island.'

But that was but a foolish lover's dream. You know all that happened since then and since the day I tried to help Will escape from Winchester Gaol. I have tried to forget all those long, long months of misery, all the agonies of my life on board the transport among the reckless and sin-hardened women whom one shuddered even to hear speak, and I did forget it all the day when I laid my face upon his bosom in a strange land, and wept as would a child when it seeks it parent's arms with the joy of knowing its sorrows are over.

And so there we were married. Little sound of bells was there, as there would have been in Solcombe Church ; only the clank of manacled felons and the harsh words of command of the soldier officers as, the ceremony over, we were marched away to our quarters to begin our lives as convicted criminals in a strange land.

The heavy tide of suffering that swept over me and mine since the first year or two of our married life has taught me many a bitter lesson ; and though our lot was then hard and cruel, and my heart was nigh to burst with the shame and indignities that befell us, yet would I endure them all again a thousand times over, for I, who suffered least, made Will's lot the harder to bear by my bitter repining and fierce temper. Not that I repined or was grieved that I had followed so far the man I loved ; but I soon began to hate with a bitter and deadly hatred our vile and horrible surroundings, and the sight of the red-coated Marines, who stood guard over Will and his fellow-prisoners from dawn till dark, as they toiled on those wild and savage shores, made my heart ache, and I sometimes felt as if I could have torn the musket from a sentry's grasp and, with Will by my side, fly into the woods or die in the attempt to regain our freedom.

But Will, brave-hearted Will, toiled steadily on, tenderly caring for me, and lightening, by his cheerful words and talk of a yet happy future, my dulled, repining heart, though he, I knew full well, suffered more than I.

Month after month passed, and day after day came——

the same ceaseless round of toil for Will ; for although, by reason of his willingness to work, and his great strength, he had became a favoured man with the Marine officers, yet he was given his full share of toil, and indeed somewhat more.

By-and-by, though, it came about that one of the Marine officers, who had known Will in the old, happy days at Solcombe, and who had ever proved a friend to him, spoke to the Governor about him, and told how that he was both a good boatman and a skilled fisherman ; and Captain Phillip, like the good, kind-hearted Gentleman he is, promised he would see to the matter and put Will to something better than hewing stone, which was then his work. In a few weeks the Governor kept his promise, and Will was given charge of a fishing boat, and ordered to live just across the ridge from Sydney Cove, where there was another small bay. Here we, with a few other prisoners, made the fishing station, and being away from the main body of prisoners we had the whole bay to ourselves, and were interfered with by no one, not even the guard of Marines who were posted between us and the rest of the settlement.

For a long while matters went on well with us. To please my dear husband I had curbed my tongue and temper, and so I, too, became somewhat of a favourite with Will's superiors, and learned the folly and harm of giving way to any outburts of temper when some one of the officers would talk to either

Will or I in a way that only the free man dare talk to a felon.

We had been quite a long time living at the Farm Cove, and my second child was about six months old when a great dearth of food afflicted us all, prisoners and free men alike, at the settlement. The country itself yielded us nothing; no food came from England as Captain Phillip had expected, and before long we soon felt what the actual pangs of hunger meant. Up till this time we had always had, at least, enough food, hard and coarse as it was, and after the Governor had placed us all on short rations, Will and his men would sometimes manage to hide a few small fish in the bosoms of their shirts for my children. But by-and-by not even this much did they dare do, for the moment the boat touched the shore their take was carefully examined and counted by some of the Marines detailed for the duty. Day by day matters grew worse, and the small ration of flour and pork served out to us had to be still further reduced; and then I had the misery of hearing my eldest child, my boy Emanuel, wail and cry for more food. Of course both Will and I stinted ourselves so that our children might have their fill, but yet the food itself was so coarse and poor that naught but the pangs of hunger would have made the poor infants cry for it. And then, in despair at the sight of their pinched and wan faces, I determined

to cast about and seek food for them myself.

Although Will and I did receive more consideration from our gaolers than any others of those
prisoners who made up the fishing settlement, we
had, in common with them, to be within doors at
sunset. Now I knew that all along the muddy
shores of the Farm Cove there lay buried in the
mud great numbers of cockles, and I had seen
Nathaniel Lilley and James Cox, two of Will's
gang, bring a basketful of them ashore one day and
roast them on a fire which had been kindled on the
beach to boil a pot of pitch. Coarse and ill-
flavoured as these things were, they were yet good
enough for hungry people, and so it was that every
night one of Will's gang would steal down to the
shore when the tide served, and, groping in the
mud with his bare hands and feet, secure enough for
me to boil late at night over a small fire. But this
had to be done with great caution, for so scarce
had food now become that had it leaked out that
these cockles were so handy to the settlement, they
would have soon been all taken ; besides this, we who
took them would have been punished for stealing.

One night, however, one of the Marines of the
guard-house near our little settlement saw someone moving about in the darkness, and challenged
and fired, and the man who had nearly filled his
basket with cockles, dropped and fled in affright to

his quarters, and then came and told Will and I of what had happened.

Much against my husband's wish I set out, and after some search found the bag and carried it to our hut, but we dared not kindle a fire that night, for fear that the guard might discover it. However, after that, as the men were frightened, I always went, and by this means was enabled to eke out our scanty supply of rations and give more of our flour to the children who, poor things, needed it sadly.

As I was returning home to our hut one evening, wet and cold, carrying a small bag half filled with these shell-fish, I heard a step behind me and then a man came up to me and placed his hand on my shoulder.

'Good evening to you, Mistress Bryant,' said he with a laugh that at once angered me. 'I watched your doings down to the shore, and as I am struck with your pretty face I made up my mind to wait for you as you came back.'

Now this man had been one of the officers of the transport which had brought me to the settlement, and during the passage he had continually thrust himself forward upon me, though it was but short and bitter speech I ever gave him. He had been given an appointment on shore by Captain Phillip, and though I did not often see him, yet whenever I did, he would always contrive to say something to me that, had Will heard it, he would have fared badly for it, not only from Will but from the Governor as well.

I turned and faced him, and asked him how he dared to stop me.

'Dare, my dear, I will dare much for such a face as yours,' and he made to me.

'Touch me at your peril, Mr ——, King's officer though you be, and I will call the sergeant of the guard,' and I struck back his hand with my pronged shell-fish stick.

This roused his evil nature, for then he told me, with a snarl, that he knew all about our stealing the shell-fish at night, and that he would report it and have us flogged. So then, in great terror, I begged his mercy and asked him to consider my feelings as a mother, for it was only because my children were starving that I was taking the shell-fish from the Cove. Finally he let me go, but only on the condition that I would meet him at some future time ; 'Otherwise,' said he, 'I. will spoil these shell-fish suppers of yours, Mistress Bryant.'

I was so terrified at the harm that this man might do us that I ran all the rest of the way to our hut, and flinging down the bag of shell-fish at Will's feet, burst into tears. And then I told him of my adventure.

It was from that night that I first conceived the idea of urging my poor Will to better our condition by escaping from the settlement altogether.

CHAPTER XXIX

THE BEGINNING OF A STRANGE AND HAZARDOUS ENTERPRISE

THE awfulness of our situation, and the life to which we were bringing up our dearly-loved children, became daily more apparent, and so this idea of mine about escaping took such possession of me that I gave my husband no peace. At first he opposed all my arguments, and declared he would not betray the trust reposed in him, but my sinful obstinacy prevailed in the end, and dearly have I paid for my wickedness.

For a long time the lack of opportunity prevented us from forming any plan of escape, but after a time chance threw in our way so many opportunities that it was not wonderful that we took advantage of them.

First it came about that John Butcher was sent to the Farm Cove. He was a prisoner who came out in the second fleet, and was a man who had been to sea and learned the art of navigating, and when I heard that he had this knowledge, I told Will that he must engage him to go with us in the boat and guide us to some country where we might earn our bread without fear of discovery, but on no account to let the others suspect our intention, lest they should betray us.

Then the Dutch ship came round to the Cove, and the master of her, a Mr Smith, took it into his head to show a partiality towards me, and this silly vanity of his I resolved to turn to the account of us all. And so it was that I encouraged him, with such arts as women understand, to believe that he had won my heart, and that for his sake I could be false to my dear, dear husband and my children. I told him many dreadful lies, and at last got him to believe that if it were possible to supply my husband with the means of escape, Will would gladly leave me to my fate, and then I could safely grant all that the Dutchman asked.

The vain fool believed my words, and actually gave me, by degrees, a good lug-sail, a compass and a quadrant, with a chart and other books such as Butcher required to steer us to Timor, which was the name of the country we had decided to try and reach. To show what a dishonest rogue the fellow was, we found that the two books he gave us did not belong to him at all, but to Captain Hunter of the *Sirius*, who was going home in the Dutchman's ship. I suppose he had stolen them from Captain Hunter's cabin, for both books had that gentleman's name written on them.

We hid these things under the boards in our hut, and then we began to collect provisions.

Just about this time a new sergeant of marines was given the charge of the guard-house at our Cove, and he noticed Smith speaking to me, and ordered me not to talk to him, because it was against the regulations. I had known this soldier, whose name was Dew, in former times, and I think he was stricter with us on that account, for he was a good man and stern soldier, and I fancy that because he was once my friend he was all the more sensible that friendship must not stand before his duty. But for all his strictness I contrived to get from Smith many useful things, besides a bag full of provisions.

The other prisoners, however, had got scent of our intentions, and although my husband feared to over-crowd the boat, and dreaded to take them with us, for some of them were very desperate men, at last, our plot having become known to them, we had to agree that they should accompany us. One of these men was anxious to take with him a woman to whom he was to have been married, but the sergeant had become very suspicious of our movements, and so my husband, who was the finest and strongest man of the party, and who was chosen leader of it, hastened our de-parture, and we left one night suddenly.

We had collected from the Dutchman, and by saving out of our scanty rations, 100 lbs. of rice, 112 lbs. of flour, 14 lbs. of pork, and 10 gallons of water.

At half-past ten, on the night of March the twenty-eighth, it being fine and the wind fair, we filed through

o

the chain by which the boat was fastened, and loading her almost to the water's edge with the stores, we all crept into her and pushed silently away, keeping close in along the southern shore, and rowing very gently with muffled oars. Just as we rounded a rocky point on the eastern side of the Farm Cove, the boat ran into a floating bush or tree, and in freeing it a branch broke off and fell upon the face of the babe at my breast. It awoke with a loud, wailing cry of terror, and the night being so still and fine, we were seized with a great fear that the sound might have reached someone on shore.

We lay perfectly still for some minutes, and then began rowing again, keeping well on the southern side of the small rocky island called Pinch Gut. The wind was directly astern of us, and there being no ships lying at anchor so far down from Sydney Cove from which we could be discerned, Will and Butcher stepped the mast and hoisted the sail and guyed out the boom so that the others could keep on rowing.

In another half an hour or so we were close to the entrance of Port Jackson, and my heart gave a bound when I looked ahead and saw the black expanse of open sea lying before us. We now felt the roll of the sea, and the oars were taken inboard, and we stood out between the black shadows of the headlands into the open ocean. At this moment Nathaniel Lilley, a noisy, excitable man, stood up, and flinging his cap overboard, cried out,—

' Hurrah for liberty and Timor ! '

'Silence, you fool!' said Will, fiercely, and he struck him in the mouth with such violence that the man was nearly sent overboard.

And so began this strange and hazardous enterprise, begotten of my folly and wickedness, and of my husband's love for me. When the day broke we were many miles away from what had been my home for three unhappy years; and my youngest child still slumbered upon my bosom.

CHAPTER XXX

A VOYAGE ALONG THE SHORES OF NEW HOLLAND

THE chart given to me by the captain of the Dutch snow is before you, and on it you will see the weary leagues we journeyed, with here and there our stopping places marked by a cross. Many and many a time, when we had run into some place of refuge on the coast, to rest our cramped and wearied limbs, and had made us a rude shelter of boughs to protect us from the burning rays of the sun, Will and Butcher, and, indeed, every one of us, would so pore and study over it, that in time we knew every line and mark and name traced upon it, and watched with great concern every fresh line pencilled upon it by our navigator.*

* *Note by Sergeant Dew.*—Take great care of this rough chart, my children. It is the only relic of this wonderful voyage, and it came into my possession through Mr Fairfax, who obtained it from Captain Edwards of the *Pandora*, to whom it was given, with various other papers concerning Bryant's party, by the captain of the Dutch ship that brought them prisoners to the Cape.

Note by the Editors.—A facsimile of the chart in the possession of Sergeant Dew's descendants is here given. It is without doubt one of Cook's earlier charts, showing the discoveries and track of the *Endeavour* in 1769 and 1770. The reader, by comparing it with a modern map of the coast line, will be able to form some idea of the remarkable boat

Our boat was so small and so deeply laden, that as soon as daylight broke on the memorable morning that followed our escape, and the breeze strengthened a little, the water began to dash over us on all sides, and we had to take to constant bailing to keep from foundering. At about ten o'clock we brought to, under the shelter of a small, high island, and made shift to effect a better disposition of the many things with which the boat was lumbered up. Butcher and some of the others wished us to land on a little beach on the lee side of the island, so that we might take out the mast and alter the sail in some way, but Will, to whom the others looked for guidance, refused, as he thought it not unlikely we might be pursued. So, without further delay, we sailed out again, and all that day continued to make good progress, even though the boat was so heavily laden and cumbersome.

At daylight next morning we were close to the entrance of a harbour, which Butcher said he thought was Port Stephens, and as we were all now suffering from the great heat, Will determined that we should put in there and rest for a day; but after we had rounded a high, conical headland, we found that there was such a great swell rolling in, and so strong a current sweeping out, that we could make

journey performed by the Bryants, and the slight knowledge of navigation possessed by Butcher. Every mile of this coast is now surveyed and charted. At the time of the Bryants' escape it was practically unknown.

no headway against it with the oars; so we had
to turn back, and hoisting our sail again, kept on
our way northwards.   After sailing for some ten or
eleven leagues, we saw the entrance of another
harbour,* and this we succeeded in reaching safely.
Here we grounded the boat on a white, sandy beach,
and Will carried myself and Emanuel and my little
Charlotte out of the boat, and made us shelter under
the trees, for we were all but perished of weakness,
and my boy cried continually from the pain of
his hands, which the cruel sun had burnt to a
deep red.

We remained at this place for five days, and I
thanked God for His goodness in bringing us there,
for Morton and John Simms, in searching the rocks
for shell-fish, found not only these, but many score
of great lobsters, which made us a bountiful repast,
though one of our party, William Allen, was like
to have died from gorging himself too heavily.

When night came on we kindled a big fire, and
while the rest of us slept two kept watch, for fear
of the Indians; and, indeed, it was well they did so,
for when it became light, we heard the sound of
voices in the woods, and looking about us discovered
four naked savages standing on a hill near by. They
carried spears in their hands, and then, after making
threatening gestures to us, disappeared down the

---

* This was Port Stephens; the first harbour spoken of was no
doubt Newcastle, or, as it was afterwards called, Port Hunter.

other side. This made us very careful during the rest of our stay, and we removed to another sleeping place further away from the woods, so as not to be surprised and cut off in the night. Our boat, too, was always loaded up in readiness for us to fly, the moment it was necessary, and sometimes, when we saw the black figures of the Indians moving about on the opposite shore, I would take my two children and 'go into the boat, which lay afloat at anchor in shallow water. All the first two days of our stay the men caught a great store of crayfish, and we used to cut off the tail part, which is full of good meat, and splitting them open, laid them upon a rough frame-work to dry in the sun. On the fifth day we found we had nearly two hundred pounds weight of this meat, and it was carefully tied up tightly, and placed on board with our other stores.

We left this place with lighter hearts for our perilous venture, and scarcely had the boat got away more than a stone's throw from the shore, when we saw some score or so of naked Indians rush down from the woods and examine our camp. Some of them threw their javelins at us, but these failed to reach us. We called this place Port Bountiful, although on our chart it was called Port Stephen, which Butcher said was wrong, for that place was ten leagues to the south.

We kept at sea for the next three days, only landing twice, to stretch our stiffened limbs and replenish

our stock of water, for although, since we had left
Port Bountiful, it rained almost unceasingly, we had
no means of catching the water.   I think it was
this constant exposure of their thinly-clad bodies that
sowed the seeds of disease in those most precious to
me, and then, besides this, it much injured our poor
store of provisions.

On the fourth day we came to a place where
there was a wide river entrance, on one side of
which was a sandy beach of great extent, and on
the other, hilly, well-grassed headlands.*   We sought
to enter this river, but perceived that the surf broke
across the entrance, and we all but capsized before
we could turn the boat round and make seawards
again.   The prospect of going, perhaps, a great
distance further north before we could find another
place of refuge, greatly disheartened Will and all of
us ; and then, to add to our troubles, the wind
suddenly turned to the north-east, and a tumultuous
sea quickly rose.   Almost in despair as to what we
should do, for the coast to the southward was very
rocky and dangerous-looking, with no sheltered beaches,
we fortunately perceived, on the southern shore of
the entrance to this river, a little indentation under
a high, conical hill.   With great skill and caution
Will and Butcher succeeded in wearing the boat
round, although at the imminent risk of our lives,
and hoisting a foot or two of the sail, we ran swiftly

* Fort Macquarie.

into the little cove and beached the boat. In quite
a short time the wind increased to a gale, and we
thanked God for our escape, for our boat could not
have lived a minute in such a furious sea that now
swept in with thundering rollers upon the coast.

Above the place where we had landed was a well-
grassed and lightly-wooded country, and as there
were no signs of Indians visible, Will and his men
hauled up the boat out of reach of the furious seas,
and we proceeded to choose a resting-place on the
flat ground above ; for Butcher said that this north-
easterly gale would last three days, and so it proved.
We made a rough protection against the fury of the
wind, and that night we all slept well save my poor
boy, who seemed to ail more and more every day.
The following day we turned our boat over and
paid her seams with tallow made from the fat of
our pork rations, and having dried our clothing, I
made a comfortable resting-place under the boat for
my infants, and sat beside them on the outside, while
Will and the others sought for lobsters on the rocks,
but found none, for the surf was still too heavy to
discern anything in the rocky pools.

The next day the wind began to moderate, but
the sea was still very mountainous, and so we were
in no hurry to leave ; besides this, my boy Emanuel
was ill of a cough that shook his poor little frame
greatly, though he never complained. Strange to
say, though, my baby began to show signs of better

health, and would laugh and crow when Will smiled or spoke to her. In the forenoon Morton, Lilley, Allen and James Cox set out along the southern shore of the river to look at the country, but they found, after going a mile or so, that it turned northward and that the water was salt. However, they discovered that a fresh-water stream with a reedy margin ran into it just where it branched off, and among these reeds they found a great many nests of wild duck, in which were eggs. These they brought back with them, and we made a very good meal, though it went to my heart to see that my poor boy ate but a morsel. Morton told me he had seen a flock of ducks swimming about on the river, and I thought that we might, perhaps, snare one and make some strengthening broth for the child, but Will said it could not be done, and so I could do naught but pray that the child might be spared to us. This place, we found, was not marked on our chart, but it was said by Butcher to be in $31\frac{1}{2}°$ of southern latitude.*

We would have stayed here a day or so longer, but that on the evening of the third day we saw many savages walking along a sandy spit on the northern side of the river, and feared to stay lest we might be surprised with the boat out of the

* Port Macquarie, at the entrance to the Hastings River, discovered and named by Oxley in 1828, lat. 31° 25′ 45″ south. The fresh-water river was Coolenbung Creek, which debouches into the Hastings near its mouth.

water.   Therefore, at sunset we once more put to
sea, and the wind now being from the east and
south, we were able to sail clear of the long, sandy
beach which lay on our left hand.   All that night,
however, it rained in squalls, and we were drenched
and shivering when the sun rose.

CHAPTER XXXI

FOR the next week or so we continued steadily onward, landing occasionally to rest and refresh our wearied bodies, the boat making good headway with a fair south-east wind; but we suffered dreadful misery from the continuous strain. We found that as we progressed northwards the savages increased in numbers and daring, so that we were soon obliged to resort to landing only as darkness came on, leaving our refuges for the night at dawn.

One of our companions, John Simms, who was also known as Samuel Bird, was a man of a very violent and intractable temper, and he was constantly lamenting that we had no muskets and ammunition with us wherewith to kill some of the Indians; but Will, who, although he was a courageous man, was no lover of bloodshed, rebuked him for his desire to shed blood needlessly. For ·this Simms gave him a saucy answer and a threatening look, and I could see that trouble was brewing, for my husband was not the man to take foul words from any man. However, he said

naught at the time, but when we were landed at
our next stopping-place, which Butcher told us was
called Glass House Bay, he waited till we had eaten
our evening meal of dried lobster and salt pork, and
had set the night watch, and rose to his feet.

'John Simms,' said he, and although he spoke
so quietly, I knew that danger was in his voice,
'this morning you told me that you were as good
a man as I. Stand up and prove it.'

With that they sprang at each other, but Simms
was no match for my Will, who struck him but
once and fractured his jaw, and then turning to
John Butcher, who stood by laughing, he reproved
him sharply. It was no laughing matter, said he,
for people in our perilous position to quarrel among
themselves. They had made him their leader, and
their leader he meant to be, unless a better man
came forward.

Now this Butcher, who is, for all his sneering
tongue and reckless manner, a man of proven
courage, thought fit to make him an answer that
brought him no good, for Will suddenly darted
out his hand, and seizing him by the throat, shook
him as a dog shakes a rat, Butcher the while
thrusting madly at him with his knife. For a
minute or so they strove madly together on the
sand, and then my husband lifted the man up with
both hands, and dashed him down violently upon
his back, where he lay stunned and motionless

beside the man with the broken jaw. But yet, after his passion was over, Will tended each of them as he would have tended a sick child, and in the morning, as we prepared to get into the boat again, John Butcher came to him and held out his hand.

'Will Bryant,' said he, 'let us be friends. You are a better man than any of us, and though I fear no man under the sun, yet, for the sake of these poor children, and Mary your wife, I ask pardon for my words of last night.'

He was a short, square-built and muscular man, with a face as dark as a Portugal, but his voice shook like a woman's when Will grasped his hand, and said in a choking voice, 'And I ask pardon of you, John Butcher; for the sake of my wife and these poor children, forgive me, comrade, for my roughness.' And with that they shook hands all round, and swore to be true to Will as long as God gave them strength to pull an oar.

In two or three days more we noticed that the sea began to get much smoother and assume a light greenish colour, and Butcher said that we had now got under the lee of the great Labyrinth Reef,* which Lieutenant Cook had discovered, and henceforth we should have smoother seas till we reached Timor. And so it proved; yet from this time we encountered many heavy gales from the south-

* The Great Barrier Reef.

east, and had to seek shelter on shore very
often.

Between the latitudes of 23° and 24° we
were driven by a strong current thirty leagues
from shore, among some islands and reefs,
where the boat was almost swamped and
lost with us all. It was nearly dark at the
time, and a squall of wind and rain struck
us suddenly with great violence, and although
we had the sail reefed, and Butcher laid the
boat to the wind, the rest of the men, except
Will, cried out that our time was come, for we
saw that we were come into a network of reefs,
upon which the sea beat with awful fury. We
tried to go about, but the boat would not stay,
and there was not room to wear. It was then
that John Butcher showed his courage and sea-
manship. In the midst of the bursting roar of
the breakers and whistling wind, and fierce, stinging rain, his voice sounded as calm and cool as it
ever did.

' 'Tis our only chance, Will, we must let go the
anchor, and try and club - haul her ; the water is
shallow enough.'

And by God's mercy the plan answered, though
as we went off on the larboard tack, a sea half
filled the boat, and drenched myself and the poor
infants to the skin. But though we had lost our
anchor we had saved our lives, and after keeping

the boat nearly with head to the wind for an hour, we found ourselves in smooth water, under the lee of a great curving reef, with clear water to leeward. Towards daylight the tide ebbed, and the boat grounded on a bottom of broken coral and sand ; and when the sun rose we saw that on the larboard hand, were numerous small, but pleasant-looking islands which, when he could look at the chart, Butcher said were the Cumberland Islands. Exhausted as we were, we put out the oars and soon rowed into a little white and sandy beach, where, to our great joy, we found large numbers of turtle. We remained here for some days, for there were no traces of savages, and dried the flesh of many turtle, so much that this addition to our store lasted us for ten days.

From this time out we passed through many clusters of islands and networks of reefs, till we came to Whit-Sunday Pass, where we landed, and thought to rest a while on a thickly-wooded island, but found it to be swarming with very savage Indians, who assailed the boat with volleys of javelins, and uttered the most dreadful cries of rage against us, so that, wearied and thirsty as we were—for our water had run out—we pushed off again hastily, and pursued our course.

All the next two days we sailed past close to the mainland, which is for the most part hereabout low and densely wooded, and with shallow, muddy foreshores. On the afternoon of the fifth day our boat sailed past Magnetical Island,* but though the place looked very inviting, we dared not land, seeing the smoke of the savages' fires ascending from the beaches in various places. Fortunately we had experienced much rain on the previous day, and had filled our small cask ; only for this we should have dared the javelins of the savages.

The wind fell light that night, and when daylight broke, had almost died away ; so we put out the oars, and rowed towards a cluster of fertile-looking islands, distant about two leagues, and which Butcher said were called the Palm Islands. And here we landed on a fair white beach, with pleasant hills in the background ; and here it was that my eldest child, my boy Emanuel, gave his innocent soul to God.

For many days before, Will and I had seen that the grey shadows of death were clouding the once bright face and sweet blue eyes of our boy, and oft at night, when our boat sped silently along under the starlit sky, I would sit holding his slight, wasted form in my arms, and my tears of repentance, for my mad and cruel folly, would fall upon his pinched and deathlike features. And, as if the dear child knew what it was that so racked my wicked heart, he would sometimes open his fast-

---

* *Note by Editors.*—Magnetic Island, a few miles from the city of Townsville, in North Queensland.

fading eyes, and his little hand would seek mine, and give it a faint pressure, and then the white lids would droop and close again. Almost as the boat touched the sand, the small, tender form trembled gently in my arms, his eyes met mine for the last time in this world, and with a sigh that stabbed me to the heart, he died.

Only that God in His mercy had yet spared to me my baby, I think that I, too, should have died on those lonely islands, for when I saw the little body of my boy placed in his sandy grave, with his small white hands crossed upon his innocent bosom, my reason left me, and I called upon God to strike me dead for the heavy sin I had done in sacrificing my first-born child.

How long we stayed on this island, which will be sacred to me till my death, I cannot tell; but I remember that even the roughest and most hardened of the men treated me very tenderly, and even wild, reckless John Butcher took my baby in his arms and pressed its face to his, and a tear stole down his dark and rugged cheek.

We left the isle at about the time of sunset, and as we sailed slowly away from the snow-white beach into the darkness, Will, who steered, put the tiller into my hand, and, covering his face, gave a great heart-breaking sob.

CHAPTER XXXII

THE FUGITIVES PASS THROUGH MANY TERRIBLE DANGERS AND ARRIVE AT COUPANG IN THE DUTCH EAST INDIES

As we sailed northward towards the Straits of Endeavour, the rainy weather that had attended us for so long in a great measure ceased, and the sun beat down upon us with painful fierceness. At this stage of our journey the long line of reef that we had had on our right hand for so many hundreds of miles now began to run closer to the mainland, and we passed through vast numbers of small islands, the most of them very low and sandy and covered with a dense verdure of shrubs ; others were of greater size and had high trees upon them. Although the wind blew very strongly from the south and east, the sea was very smooth, for the great reef that was now only a few leagues distant proved an excellent barrier to the violence of the ocean waves. The coast hereabout was for the most part long stretches of beach, with dense forests behind it and a range of very high mountains further inland.

We seldom ventured to land on the mainland now, for the Indians were very numerous, and at night time we could see their fires at frequent intervals all along the beaches, and on the summit of the headlands. The navigation, too, was very difficult, so at night time we generally put ashore on one of the small, sandy islets, and choosing a spot sheltered from the wind, passed the night in some degree of comfort; though even here there was danger from the savages, who resorted to these places for fishing, as we often met them crossing to and fro between these islands and the mainland in small canoes.

On one occasion, though, when we were come to Cape Flattery, we had to land on the mainland to seek for water, which Butcher said we would find there; and here we had like to all have perished miserably by the savages. We had found the water, and were ready to put off again, when the tide ebbed and the boat grounded, and then great numbers of Indians appeared on some rocks that jutted down on to the beach near us and assailed us with stones and javelins. Many of their javelins came into the boat and stuck into her timbers, but by God's mercy none of us were struck, and we all, except myself, got out into the sea and so lightened the boat that we were able to drag her out into deeper water, and so escape. When we were getting our water at this place we saw many serpents about the beach and rocks, and even on the sea we met with them constantly swimming about. But Butcher told us that these water serpents were not venomous, and were indeed but a scaly eel, yet they had a very horrible appearance. On the beaches, and about the muddy shores of the mainland, there were also visible many huge crocodiles lying basking in the sun.

When we had come close to Cape Weymouth, we saw from the boat that there appeared to be water trickling down the face of some reddish-coloured rocks, and so, the landing looking easy of accomplishment, and there being no signs of Indians, Will put ashore at the end of the beach near the rocks, where we found water collected in small, rocky pools at the foot of the cliffs, but no stream or river. All along this beach we found great piles of large, curved bones, built up in the shape of mounds. What the animal was that these bones came from we could not tell ; but it was easy to see that the mounds had been placed there by the savages, for on the tops of some of them were the shells of very large turtles.* We spent the earlier part of the day resting at this place, and began our voyage at noon. To avoid the strong current we kept in close to the shore, and while sailing along we passed numbers of sea-cows feeding on the shallows ; but having no weapon of any sort, could not kill one to replenish our now exhausted stock of food.

We made good progress until we reached Cape

* *Note by Editors.*—The practice still prevails, among the savage natives of the far North Queensland coast, of piling up mounds of dugong bones, surmounted by a turtle carapace, at regular intervals ; the reason for so doing has never been discovered.

Granville, where, although we saw many signs of Indians about, we were forced to land for water and search for food. My baby now began to ail for want of strengthening food; so while four of our party remained with me in the boat, which we moored within a short distance of the shore, the others set out to search for turtle and shell-fish. In a few hours they returned with a great quanity of gar-fish, which they had caught in a shallow pool, and James Cox brought with him a number of young, unfledged birds, which he had taken from their parents' nests in the woods. These we made a broth from by kindling a fire and heating stones, which were dropped into a tiny pool in the rocks. By doing this several times, the young birds, which had been cut in pieces, were boiled, and some of the broth, which was very strong and nutritious was given to my infant, a spoonful at a time. To my great joy little Charlotte drank it eagerly and soon began to mend, and so we saved all that was left for her, and put it in a gourd which we had found on the beach at Cape Weymouth. As for the flesh of the young birds, we ate that ourselves, and then it came out from Cox that he had eaten a number of them raw in the woods. This so angered Will and Butcher that Cox sprang to his feet in fear and ran back into the woods. We thought he had deserted us, but in half an hour he came back stripped to the waist and carrying something heavy in his shirt, which was tied at the sleeves and neck so as to form a bag.

Casting it down on the rocks besides us, we perceived that it was filled with dead birds, both young and old, the last about the size of a gull. He told us that when he had first found the birds his hunger had so overpowered him that he ate ravenously of nearly twenty, and that he had meant to tell us that there were many more in the same place after we had eaten those we had boiled; whereupon we forgave him. Cox, Will and myself now set to and plucked many of the birds, which we cooked by hot stones in a large, round hole in the rock, filled with water, and we all ate most heartily again. Later on two of the men set out again for more, and found a great rookery of many thousands of these birds just over the brow of the hill. They caught and killed nearly three hundred of the old birds, for the poor things would not desert their offspring.

At this place also we saw many herds of sea-cows feeding in the shallows between some sand-spits, but could not kill any. However, we drew the seine and caught a vast quantity of fish. These we split and hung up to dry in the wind and sun; and although we feared a visit from the Indians, Will decided to remain at this spot for another day or two, as my baby was gaining strength every hour through the broth that we gave her every now and then.

On the third day at sunrise, with a great store of dried fish and half-cooked birds, we began our voyage again, and at dusk Will bore up for a small island distant about five miles from the main, for we feared to sail on at night by reason of the darkness and many reefs. Here, to our great joy, we found a number of turtle and caught five; two of these were of so great a size that each took the strength of four men to lift it. That night it blew very hard, and we had to unload the boat and haul her up on the beach. We then crept into the centre of the thicket on the island, and so passed the night. At daylight we found that many turtle had been ashore during the night, and laid a vast number of eggs; so many, indeed, that the shell of the largest turtle we had caught could not hold them all. I beat up the yolks of some of the eggs and gave this mixture to little Charlotte, who drank it with great relish. We got away by noon from here.

We were now close to the Straits of Endeavour, and so thickly was our way studded with islets, reefs and shoals, that we had always to land at night and wait for daylight. Sometimes we suffered severely from the swarms of mosquitoes which were very numerous, and would not even be driven away by smoke.

Just before we rounded York Cape,* which is the last headland on the coast of New South Wales, we landed on the mainland for water and filled our casks at a large fresh-water river, and here some

* Cape York.

of our party suffered great bodily agony by touching the leaves of a tree. It seems that Nathaniel
Lilley, James Cox and William Morton spied, walking about in a thicket, a great bird covered with
black hair and with a horned head,* and thinking
to catch it, they all three gave chase. In about
half an hour they returned in great agony, and
said that in chasing the bird they had brushed
against the leaves of trees with large, glossy leaves,
very beautiful and harmless to look at, but wher-
ever these leaves had touched their skins they soon
began to feel as if red-hot irons had seared their
flesh. Indeed, they were in such dreadful pain that
night that Lilley was quite out of his senses, and
the others almost as bad; and the pains continued
for a long time after.†

We rounded York Cape with a strong wind from
the E.S.E., and brought to for the night in a little
bay on the western side, so as to stow our boat better
for the voyage across the open sea to Timor, which
Butcher said was nearly straight to the westward
from York Cape.

That night we rowed the boat to a sandbank
some distance from the shore, for we saw many
Indians armed with spears watching us from the
mainland. There was much driftwood on the

---

* A Cassowary.

† *Note by Editors.*—The coastal scrubs of Northern Queensland are
infested with the stinging-tree, the slightest contact of the leaves of
which with the human skin causes the most excruciating pain.

sandbank, and we lit a fire, and then, after we had
eaten our evening meal of dried flesh and drank our
allowance of water, Butcher and Will spread out the
Dutchman's chart on the sand.   We all gathered
round in silence, and then when Butcher showed
us the vast open space of ocean we had yet to pass
over before we reached Timor, our hearts sank within us.   But Will and Butcher cheered us up by
telling us that although three hundred leagues was
a long way, yet, as we should not have many
places to touch at, we should reach Timor all the
sooner.   So with that we were content, though that
night none of us slept ; for we could hear the savages
making a great outcry on the mainland, and feared
they might come off in canoes and attack us.

It was in Will and Butcher's minds for us to steer
due west for Timor, but for the fear that if we met
with foul winds our water might give out ; so instead of this we steered west and by south, so as to
cross a great gulf shown on the chart,* touched on
the coast of New Holland again to replenish our
provisions and water, and then steered a north-
westerly course to Timor.

I will not here tell of all our further sufferings,
but will bring the account of our voyage to an end.
We crossed the gulf safely and found abundance
of turtle, fish and water on the coast on the
other side, which we followed, I think, for about

* The Gulf of Carpentaria.

fourteen or fifteen days before we finally left it.
This part of New Holland is truly a dreadful
country, for all the shores are muddy and full of
crocodiles, and the woods infested with serpents;
and though we saw but few Indians here, we
were often chased by a new race of savages, in
large canoes, fitted with sails and great fighting
stages, and sometimes holding thirty men in each.*
These we escaped by rowing hard to windward,
and so with such adventures, and with my poor Will
suffering from a malignant fever, which came upon
him the day we left the coast, and my little
Charlotte ailing from want of nourishment, we at
last reached Coupang, the name of the Dutch
settlement at Timor, more dead than alive.

* *Note by Editors.*—Evidently Malay prahus, which have, since the
very early history of Australia, voyaged to its northern shores.

CHAPTER XXXIII

A VERY HEAVY PUNISHMENT IS METED OUT TO
MARY, AND THE FUGITIVES AGAIN BECOME
PRISONERS

WE reached Coupang on the fifth of June, and landed
there in the afternoon. There was a great assemblage
of both white and black people to see us land, and I
have no doubt but that our appearance was very strange
and deplorable. The skins of nearly every one of us
was burnt to a dark brown colour, and Butcher, Lilley,
and William Morton looked more like wild animals
than human beings. As for me, I was very weak, and
could scarcely hold my little Charlotte in my arms,
and poor Will, who was now suffering terribly from the
fever and violent shivering fits, which came on him
every few hours, had to be carried out of the boat.

As soon as we were landed, the Dutch people were
very kind to us, and we gave out that our party were
the survivors of an English vessel wrecked on her way
to Port Jackson from the coast of America, and also
added, which was true enough, that we had been in
the boat for ten weeks all but one day. Butcher, we
said, was one of the officers, and Will and I were
passengers.

The Dutch governor, Timotheus Wangon, Esquire, treated us all very well, and sent a doctor to attend upon Will. He also sent an Indian woman to attend upon me and little Charlotte, and provided me with some wine and a baked fowl for my immediate wants ; the rest of the men were also given good food, and a change of clothes was brought to each by a Dutch soldier.

Perhaps all would have gone well with us after all, but, after we had been at Coupang nearly three months, Butcher and Morton and John Simms, who were lodged in a house near the soldiers' quarters, were one night talking over our escape, and by-and-by, their tongues being loosened by some drams of an ardent spirit given to them by one of the soldiers, they got careless and talked very loudly. Presently there came outside the house a Dutch merchant captain and a Dutch trader from Ternate, who, it seems, both spoke English, and had come to visit the shipwrecked English sailors out of curiosity. But these two had heard a word or two fall from Butcher which made them wait outside and listen for more, and they soon heard enough to convince them that we were escaped convicts from Botany Bay. So away they went to the Governor and told him.

This happened on the twenty-ninth of August, and, strange to say, it was on that very day that there reached Coupang, Captain Edwards and the crew of the *Pandora*, a King's ship which had been cast away

on the coast of New Holland. Among them were
also some prisoners, part of the mutineer crew of
Lieutenant Bligh's ship. It seems that when Mr
Bligh had reached England, the Government had sent
out the *Pandora* to search for these mutineers, and
they had been found and seized at an island in the
South Seas. Three or four of them had perished
miserably in their irons when the *Pandora* went
down, the rest were brought to Coupang. As soon
as Captain Edwards heard the story of the Dutch
Governor about us being suspected as escaped convicts,
he got Mr Wangon to have us seized, and in a very
brief time we were all, save myself, seized, heavily
ironed, and cast into prison with the men from the
Bounty.

Poor Will, who was still in a very weak state, only
had time to kiss me and little Charlotte farewell, when
he was torn from me, and taken with the others, and
I, distracted woman that I was, was put into a prison
apart from him.

In a few days the King's officer chartered a ship
belonging to the Dutch East India Company, and
named the *Hornwey*, to take us with his ship's company, and the other prisoners, to Batavia, from where
he hoped to get another ship to take us to the Cape of
Good Hope.

And so, once more with clanking irons upon their
fettered limbs, my unfortunate companions in misery
were placed on board the Dutch ship. I was not

placed in irons myself by that stern and cruel King's officer, but with my child in my arms was allowed to sit down on the main deck of the ship, so that I was at least near my dear husband. The Dutch sailors were kind to me, and one managed to get the sentry over us to turn away his head while he slipped a bottle of milk into my hand for little Charlotte, who could not understand why her father sat there with his face bowed upon his knees, and tried to crawl over to him.

To me that voyage in the *Hornwey* was a very dreadful one. I could see that my husband was dying before my eyes, and yet could not even go near him to pillow his weary head upon my breast, for the sentry had orders not to let me speak to any of my companions—no, not even my own dear Will.

One night the *Hornwey* lay becalmed. It was very dark and hot, and even in the open air we poor prisoners could scarce breathe. There was not a sound to be heard, save the grating of the prisoners' irons upon the deck when they moved their aching limbs. Presently I saw James Cox, who had been very quiet and sad all day, rise upon his knees, and moving very gently so that the sentry could not hear him, crawl up to Will and whisper a word or two in his ear, and their manacled hands met for a minute. Then looking round to where I lay upon a grating, he beckoned me to him. I crept over, carrying my baby with me.

'Mistress Bryant,' said he in a whisper, 'give me your hand. I shall be a dead man before morning.'

'Don't say that, James,' I said ; 'see how my poor Will bears up, ill as he is.'

'Mistress Bryant, 'tis better for us all to die as soon as we can. But give me your hand, good woman, and hush ! make no noise, but give me the brat to kiss.'

I held my sleeping baby's face to his, and he pressed his lips to her forehead, and then he suddenly raised himself erect, and his chains making a great noise, clambered to the ship's side and sprang overboard. May God forgive me his death !

There was a great outcry made, but, of course, the poor man had sunk like a stone ; so no boat was lowered. But that the others might not follow his example, they were chained to ringbolts in the deck. That night a very furious storm burst upon us with terrible rain, and in the morning William Morton lay dead and stiff in his irons. He was never a very strong man, and the sufferings he had undergone in the boat had quite broken his health, even as it had Will's. And soon after, John Simms followed him. He died very quietly, and, indeed, we did not know he was dead till the sentry called to him to look up, as Captain Edwards was coming. But the man made no answer, and Will, who was next to him, said to the sentry in a weak voice,—

'He can't look up—not even for a King's officer— he has just breathed his last.'

At last we reached Batavia, and here I was to feel that God's hand is indeed heavy to those who sin as I have sinned.

Will was now so weak that even our stern superiors took pity on him, and he was sent to the soldiers' hospital, where I was allowed to go with him. It was a long, narrow building with a thatched roof, and though the furnishing was very poor, it was yet neat and clean. He was placed upon a pallet, and a Dutch doctor, who spoke some English, came and looked at him.

'Are you his wife?' he said to me kindly, and he motioned me to bring a wooden stool and sit near the bed. Then he whispered to me that he would not last long.

I did not think that Will had heard him, but he did, for his poor, wasted hand sought mine, and he spoke.

'Mary, my girl . . . God keep you, for I shall soon be gone. 'Tis hard to die thus, dear wife . . . to leave you and the little one.'

I sought to answer him through my tears, and bending down kissed his lips, and in his dear eyes I saw that the dark shadows of death were gathering fast, and that his breath came very slowly after each word he spoke.

At the foot of the bed stood a Dutch sergeant who, at a sign from the doctor, placed a cup of wine to his lips. He drank and then lay back again, but his eyes turned to me so piteously, that as I held his hand in mine I could not see his face for my tears. He pressed my hand tenderly, and then turning to the doctor begged to be allowed to see little Charlotte, whom I had not been permitted to bring into the hospital.

The good doctor nodded to the sergeant, and the soldier went out and brought in an Indian wench who carried the child in her arms.

'Mary, my wife, come here, dear one,' said Will to me, and he tried to smile ; 'place the little one in my arms,' but even as he spoke, and I gave the infant into his weak arms, the tears of her father gathered in his eyes and ran down his cheeks. For a moment or so he lay quiet with the child's cheek pressed to his, and his gaunt, bony arms clasped gently round her little body. Then, with one last look of love for me, he gave a heavy sigh and died.

And so God punished me.

The next day Captain Edwards hired the *Rambang*, a Dutch vessel, which brought us to the Cape of Good Hope.

And so we wretched ones who remain were brought on board this ship, and now, all I ask is that when we reach England, and my just punishment by the laws of man shall begin, that my remaining infant may be cared for and preserved from such a fate as has befallen me. I ask, too, that those of my companions who remain may be dealt with mercifully, since 'twas I, and I alone, who have brought them to this sad pass.

CHAPTER XXXIV

I ARRIVE IN ENGLAND

THIS was Mary Bryant's story, and it is told to you almost in her own words. Her petition that her infant daughter might be saved from the prison taint that she knew was awaiting her, was altered before this statement was handed to the Home Authorities, for the child Charlotte died at sea on the sixth of May, and we consigned her tiny form to the deep.

From that day we saw little of Mary, who was too ill even to come upon deck and take the fresh air. The remainder of the voyage was without interest, and the *Gorgon* arrived at Chatham on June the nineteenth, 1792, and once more I was back in my native land.

'Twas a sad sight to us to see the prisoners passed over the side of the ship on that memorable day of our arrival. First there were the miserable persons who had taken part in the mutiny of the *Bounty*, most of them, as they left the ship, never hoping, for a moment, that anything but death awaited them, though I am glad to say young Heywood, the youngest of them all, escaped, and afterwards served with great distinction on a King's ship.

Then the survivors of the Bryant party were taken in charge by the Bow Street officers, to be conveyed to London. Mary gave one look behind at the Marines, who were drawn up on the quarter-deck for inspection before disembarking.

She caught sight of Lieutenant Fairfax and myself, and waved to us a sad farewell, and though the discipline of the Service is very strict, I could not help waving my hand from where I stood, on the right flank of my company, and as I did so, I saw Major Ross look at me as if in wonder why so steady a man could so far forget himself as to signal to a convict from the ranks. But he said nothing, this being so great an occasion, and perhaps he had caught sight of Lieutenant Fairfax, who lowered the point of his sword ever so little, but still enough for Mary to see that he intended this signal of farewell for her.

As soon as we were landed we were marched off to the depôt at Chatham, and after a few days we, who returned from Port Jackson, were granted a long furlough, and joyously departed for our homes.

Lieutenant Fairfax sent for me the last thing before I left, and said he,—

'Now, Dew, I cannot, I am sorry to say, return with you by the coach to Portsmouth; but remember this, when you get back to dear old

Solcombe—that is, if you've a mind to it, and have had enough of the Service—when I leave London it will be for good, and I will bring with me your discharge.'

I was overjoyed to hear my good patron had not forgotten his promise, and I thanked him heartily.

'Tell my sister when you give her this letter,' went on the lieutenant, handing me a bulky package, 'that I am going to remain in London until I can get clear of the Service, and while I am there I shall leave no stone unturned to soften the lot of her former maid, Mary Bryant.' Here he turned his face away from me for a moment. 'Now be off with you and get all in readiness to turn farmer, for there is no more pipeclay for either of us.'

When I reached Portsmouth in the coach, I purchased a newspaper to take over to my father at the island. For I had seen by the advertisement outside of the printing-house, as we drove up in the coach, that it contained a publication which the printers entitled, 'Strange Story of an Escape from Botany Bay.'

So I bought a copy of the *Hampshire Chronicle and Portsmouth and Chichester Journal*, and there I read, with much emotion, a full account of Mary's appearance at Bow Street Police Court in London.

It set forth that on Saturday last, which was the fifteenth of July, Sir Sampson Wright's officers brought up at the Police Court five prisoners from

His Majesty's frigate *Gorgon*, and then with many errors, such as newspapers so often contain, it related the story of the Bryants' escape. The person who reported the matter wrote,—'It was remarked by everyone present, and by the magistrate, that they never saw people who bore stronger marks of a sincere repentance, and all joined in the wish that their past sufferings may be considered as a sufficient expiation of their crimes. They all declared that they would sooner suffer death than return to Botany Bay. They were committed to Newgate.'

CHAPTER XXXV

BEFORE I left Chatham, I had received a letter from your Aunt Dorothy, telling me that she had been wedded to that honest yeoman, your Uncle John, just about the time that we were leaving the Cape of Good Hope in the *Gorgon*.

She had tried to persuade her husband to postpone the happy event until my return to England, that I might dance at the wedding, but he would not listen to this, 'for,' said he, 'the *Gorgon* took long enough getting to Botany Bay to fetch your brother, and if we wait until she returns with him, we may be too old for thoughts of marriage before he gets to England;' and, indeed, he spoke most sensibly.

And so they were married, and your aunt went away to live at her new home on the other side of the island, and my father was left to the care of the woman who helped in the household.

Alas! my home-coming was not so joyful as I had anticipated, for when I landed on Ryde beach from the Portsmouth wherry, a waterman, who was lounging about, came up to me and said,—

'I say, you, soldier, ain't you young Sergeant Dew from Botany Bay?'

'I am that man,' I answered.

'Well,' said he, 'you don't remember me, but I am a near neighbour of yours over by Solcombe, and they are looking forward anxiously for you to come back. Your old father is very ill, and I am afraid you won't see him alive.'

And so, on hearing this sad news I hastened away, and getting into a farmer's cart that was going that way, without waiting for the carrier, I got as far as Newport, and from there walked to my home.

Sure enough, I found your aunt and uncle and the doctor, and all of them around the bedside of my father, who, after recovering consciousness, and giving me his blessing and forgiveness for all the anxiety I had caused him, closed his eyes for ever, and left me the lonely master of our little farm.

I did all things decently, and buried your grandfather in the parish churchyard, following his remains in my scarlet tunic with a crape band round my arm, the neighbours, who followed from the country side for a long way round, all staring at me, and some of them, no doubt, pointing me out as an example of a young man who had been a rolling stone. Miss Charlotte Fairfax sent her chaise to follow at the funeral, and I felt the honour very much.

I had sent her brother's letter to her with my

best respects, and told her of my father's illness, and
that, as soon as I could leave him, I would present
my duty, and begged to be granted an interview.

She very graciously replied that I was to suit my
own time and convenience, and now that all was
over, I resolved to call upon her.

Accordingly, one day I walked over to the Manor,
and was shown into the drawing-room.

Miss Fairfax lived all alone, managing the estate
for her brother, with the aid of a bailiff, and an old
lady lived with her as a sort of companion and
housekeeper.

I found Mary's mistress very little altered in appearance, and, as I have told you, she was a great beauty ;
but she was much sobered in her manner, and had
the air and conversation of a much older woman.

She was very gracious to me, and addressed me as
Mr Dew. After her first greeting, said she :—'But,
Mr Dew, why do you appear thus in your uniform ?
It becomes you mightily, but, goodness me, we are
not at war in the island, Heaven be thanked.'

'If you please, Miss Fairfax,' I answered, 'the
humbler ranks of the military, and the Marines also,
are allowed no other dress ; and, indeed, madam, I
have no other clothes but these.'

'Ah, then,' and she smiled most prettily, 'you
have not heard from my brother. He tells me, Mr
Dew, in a letter which was delivered to me only
to-day, that he himself is now released from the King's

Service, and he has also procured your discharge from the Marines.'

I was mightily pleased to hear this, as you may be sure, and so I said, and expressed my gratitude.

Then Miss Fairfax, who seemed to grow more beautiful every minute, requested me to tell her of the strange adventures of the Bryants; and so I told their story as you have heard it, and her eyes filled with tears, and then the tender-hearted lady turned her face from me and wept softly to herself a while.

When she had recovered herself, and dried her pretty eyes, she was so condescending as to make me stay and take a dish of tea with her and her old lady companion in the drawing-room; and I felt myself a very high and important person, I can tell you, as I walked away home to begin life as a tenant farmer on my small estate, and one of the principal persons in our neighbourhood.

CHAPTER XXXVI

MR FAIRFAX PAYS A FLYING VISIT, AND JOHN BUTCHER SENDS IN A PETITION

You may depend upon it that I was well pleased, on getting back to my farm, to receive a letter from my old master, enclosing in it my formal discharge from the Service. In this letter he told me that he was working hard to obtain mercy for poor Mary and the unhappy survivors of the boat voyage. He also wrote that he would not be back in Solcombe for some time to come, as he had many things to attend to in London. Then he asked me to give his sister a helping hand with the Solcombe estate, as she, being a lone woman dependent upon a bailiff, would be glad of my advice. Of course, I was proud and pleased at this commission, and in consequence of it I was very often at the Manor, and Miss Fairfax was so good as to make much use of me; and, indeed, treated me as if I had been in all ways her equal.

Two or three months passed like this, and then we had a flying visit from Mr Fairfax. Miss

Charlotte had reproached him for not coming to see her, and he took coach and boat, and came down to the island quite unexpectedly. After a few hours spent with his sister, he was so good as to walk over to my farm.

I thanked him very heartily for remembering his old servant in the way he had done, and enabling me to settle down and become a respected man again. In reply to my words, he said, 'Now, Dew, once for all let us drop this master and servant business. I have become an extreme Whig, and hope to sit for the island yet as such. I believe all men and women are equal so far as position goes ; it is honesty and that alone which should rank us ; and now that both of us have left the Service, let us drop it. I think you are as good a man as I am, and Mary Bryant is as good a woman as my sister is. What do you think of that now ? '

This shocked me very much, and so I ventured on the liberty of saying that such sentiments did more honour to his heart than to his head. 'Why, sir,' said I, 'it is bad enough to make the servant equal to the master, but to compare Miss Fairfax with her maid—a convicted—'

'That will do, Dew,' he replied, in the old way, 'let me hear no more of such talk. I am afraid you will always be a fool in some ways.'

Then he went on to tell me that he had taken up his residence for a time, at least, in London, and he was working hard to obtain Mary's release, and hoped to do so before very long. Meanwhile, I was to look well after his sister and help her all I could. 'For, look you, Dew,' said he, 'she will want all your assistance, because I don't like farming, and will have nothing to do with it, and so I have told her.'

'This will make her very unhappy,' said I, 'for, to be sure, she must have looked forward to your home-coming, to take your place among the island gentry.'

'Oh, no, she is quite happy, and likes the idea of having you about to advise her. Good-bye,' and with a hearty hand-shake my old master walked off, leaving me somewhat dazed at the strange sentiments he had expressed.

A few weeks after this I got a copy of the Portsmouth paper, and in it I read that all the prisoners, except Mary Bryant and Butcher, had been sent to complete their sentences, but Mary Bryant's case was still under consideration. The following letter was also published in this paper from Butcher :—

'JOHN BUTCHER to the Right Hon. HENRY DUNDAS.

'NEWGATE, 23d *January* 1793.

'MAY IT PLEASE YOUR HONOUR,—It ill becomes a person, in the low sphere I move in, to address a person of your exalted character, nor should I have presumed to take the liberty but for the following reason :—Having been brought up in the thorough knowledge of all kinds of land, and capable of bringing indifferent lands to perfection, I had an offer some time ago to go to Botany Bay, to endeavour to make that land more fertile than it has ever appeared to be. I submit the following list to your honour's perusal of what is necessary seed, and what has been tried and found not to answer the expectations formed of them. Two sorts of English wheat; barley, rye and beans, one sort; grass is a good production, as likewise Indian corn; and some of the land will produce tobacco, and, all sorts of garden stuff, with proper instructions. But according to the manner in which they till the ground at present, they will bring nothing to perfection, owing to the different sorts of land in the island, which they are entirely ignorant of; and I flatter myself, from what I have seen of the island, that I could render it a great deal more productive, and, in a few years, could save the Government a great expense in provisions for the colony.

'Although I have suffered a great deal in going and coming from Botany Bay, yet I am willing to go back again on proper terms, as I am certain I can be of very great service to the island in what I profess, and if your honour should think me worthy of the situation, I am willing to place myself, and I will be bound to perform everything I undertake, or expect nothing for my trouble. I should be humbly thankful to your honour if you would condescend to indulge me with an answer, that I may know what I am to expect; you will give great ease to the anxious mind of, hon. sir, your humble servant,

'JOHN BUTCHER.'

I may as well dispose of Butcher at once, by telling you that the petition of this man was granted, and he was allowed to enlist in the New South Wales Regiment, and was sent back to the settlement. He was, in September, 1795, granted 25 acres of land in the Petersham district near Sydney, and became a flourishing settler.

CHAPTER XXXVII

I HEAR GOOD NEWS AT LAST

TIME passed on, and more months went by before we —I mean dear Miss Fairfax and myself—heard anything of her brother, my lieutenant, as I still always thought of him, although we had occasional letters from him in which we heard that he was a regular visitor to Newgate Prison, and that he had procured many indulgences for Mary, who was now quite restored to health, and sent her loving duty to her former mistress, and her kind remembrances to myself.

We had news, too, from Port Jackson. Lieutenant King had again taken charge of Norfolk Island, and that settlement was flourishing under his wise rule. This gentleman was on his way out from England, as we were returning home in the *Gorgon*, and by his personal efforts with the Government during his short stay in England, had done a great deal for the new country. Major Ross, my old commandant, became recruiting officer at the depôt, where, I have no doubt, he turned out some good soldiers to serve their King and country ; for although I cannot say I ever liked so stern and hard a Gentleman, yet he was an excellent officer—but yet I was very glad to get away from him.

Governor Phillip, so my lieutenant wrote, left the settlement in the *Atlantic* on the eleventh of December, 1792, and arrived in England in the summer of 1793, and in July of that year he resigned his post, and Sydney—for so the settlement is now called—lost the best and bravest Gentleman that ever stepped foot into it. After he left, two officers of the New South Wales Regiment—which to my mind was a very indifferent body of men when compared to my old corps—in turn became Governors ; these were Colonel Gore and Captain Patterson, and then, early in 1794, Captain Hunter, with whom I had sailed so often, was appointed Governor ; but all this is history which you can read for yourselves.

As I have said, things went on very much as usual with us at Solcombe, until, on the twenty-eighth of May 1793, I read in the Portsmouth paper this very startling piece of news :—

'His Majesty has been graciously pleased to grant a free pardon to Mary Bryant, who, accompanied by several male convicts, escaped from Botany Bay, and traversed upwards of three thousand miles by sea in an open boat, exposed to tempestuous weather.'

This was joyful news, but in another part of the paper I read something which I could have robbed of the mystery which the printer seemed to think surrounded it. This is what he wrote :—

'The female convict who made her escape from Botany Bay and suffered the greatest hardships during a voyage of three thousand leagues, and who was afterwards retaken and condemned to death, has been pardoned and released from Newgate. In the story of this woman there is something extremely singular. A gentleman of high rank in the Army visited her in Newgate, heard the details of her life, and for that time departed. The next day he returned, and told the old gentleman who keeps the prison that he had procured her pardon, which he showed him, at the same time requesting that she should not be apprised of the circumstance. The next day he returned with his carriage, and took off the young woman, who almost expired with excess of joy.'

You may well imagine that I was pleased enough to read this, although all that was printed was not strictly true ; but I knew very well that Mary was pardoned, and that my master had succeeded, and so I cared nothing for the rest.

By the same boat that brought to the island the Portsmouth papers, came letters from Mr Fairfax to his sister and myself, confirming the news of Mary's pardon, and telling us that he would soon pay us a visit, and bring us all particulars and much that would interest us.

Miss Fairfax was as pleased as myself at hearing the news, and wrote a very kind letter, which before sending she read to me, offering to take Mary back to her service, and telling her brother that now the goodness of his heart had succeeded in procuring Mary's pardon, 'twas time for him to return to the island and settle on his estate, 'for,' she said, 'although Mr Dew hath been, and is still, of very great service to me, and is most anxious to help me all in his power, yet 'tis cruel that I should be so hard upon his time and good-nature. So do you hasten back, my dear brother.'

CHAPTER XXXVIII

MR FAIRFAX SURPRISES ME VERY MUCH, AND I
BEGIN TO ASSOCIATE WITH PEOPLE OF QUALITY

Two months had gone by and we had heard nothing
more of the lieutenant, save from a short note which
he had written to Miss Fairfax, telling her not to
expect him for some weeks. Three weeks had passed
since this letter came, and both Miss Fairfax and I
wondered at hearing nothing further, when one day
I received a message to say that Mr Fairfax wanted
me at the Manor House. Before setting out I spent
some little time over my attire, as since I had begun
to see Miss Fairfax so often, I deemed it proper that I
should dress in a more befitting manner than that
which I had been accustomed to. Indeed, on Mr
Fairfax's advice, I had had two suits made in
Southampton by his own tailor, and Miss Fairfax had
told me that they became me very well. I was
never a vain man, but, of course, I could not help
knowing that, as far as looks and build went, there
were few men in the island to whom Providence had
been kinder ; and, indeed, as I was now in a comfort-

able position I began to try and improve myself in other ways by reading and paying strict attention to my deportment when in the society of Miss Fairfax. So, being very handsomely dressed in one of my new suits, which had cost each two pounds sterling, I set out, and reaching the Manor House was shown into the drawing-room.

There, in the middle of the room, stood my master, holding by the hand Mary, who looked so beautiful again that I at first scarce knew her. As I entered the room he stepped forward, and still holding Mary by the hand, said,—

'Here you are, friend Dew, come and be introduced to my wife, your old acquaintance, Mary.'

I was so astonished by this wonderful event being revealed to me in this sudden manner, that I stood stock still like a fool and said nothing. Then my old master, after waiting a moment, clapped me on my back and said, 'Come, Will Dew, won't you congratulate me?'

I really must have lost my senses, for I stood to attention just as in the old days, and saluted, and only muttered, as if I were giving the countersign on sentry duty, 'Yes, sir, I congratulate you.'

Mr Fairfax laughed outright at me, and said, 'Hang me if I don't believe you're jealous.'

Then Mary held out her hand to me, and said she, ---'No, no, Mr Dew is very much surprised that his old friend and dear master could so have forgotten his rank to take compassion upon poor me, and let his pity grow to a love so great that he could make me his wife ; and, indeed, well may he be astounded at the news.'

I had taken her hand and was still silent, looking now in her face and seeing therein a look of quiet happiness such as I had never seen before ; and now I realised that all that she had suffered had not altered her, and she was still a beautiful woman, a woman, indeed, that any man might well be proud to call his own.

Presently I recovered my wits and began to see that after all, though my rich and well-born master had committed what many persons might call a great piece of folly, and what I knew showed extraordinary freedom of prejudice on his part, yet Mary was, as I had known in the old days, far above the common rustic, and she looked and talked like a lady born.

By-and-by we grew more composed, and fell a-talking, and I noticed Miss Fairfax was not in the room and did not come in, though we were a long time together ; and so I asked Mr Fairfax if his sister had seen Mary.

He took me on one side and said,—' Yes, and there's the devil to pay. My sister has sworn never to forgive either of us, and has shut herself up in her room, where she swears she will remain until she can get another home.'

At this I expressed my sorrow that this marriage

was to be the means of Miss Fairfax leaving the
Manor.

'Oh, that will be all right,' said Mr Fairfax.
'Mary and I are going away to London this afternoon, where we shall live for years, and my sister
will remain here. You see, Dew, I am proud of my
wife, but I know and she knows, well enough, that all
the people about here will not take kindly to our
marriage at first. You know they have not seen
the world as we have, and so, like my sister, they
will have foolish prejudices, and so we are going to
live in London for a time. Meanwhile, do you look
after my sister and help her all you can, and try to
overcome her silly objections to my marriage.'

And then I said farewell to them both, and they
went away and remained in London for some years,
until the lieutenant was father of three children, whose
honoured names you know well enough.

All this time I remained a lonely man at my farm,
with no companions save the old woman who kept
house for me, and occasional visits from my sister and
her family. Now and then I would spend an evening
in the best parlour of the inn at Solcombe with the
persons of quality who frequented it, for I was now a
man of substance, all things prospering with me.

I still continued to be invited by Miss Fairfax to
the Manor House, and she very frequently challenged
me to a game of backgammon, and occasionally,
accompanied by her old lady companion, she would

ask me to escort them for a walk along the cliffs. These days were very bright spots in my life, and consoled me greatly for the quiet existence I led at the farm.

CHAPTER XXXIX

MISS FAIRFAX OUTDOES HER BROTHER IN SURPRISING
ME, AND A VERY GREAT AND HAPPY EVENT
BRINGS MY STORY TO AN END

AND now, as I draw near to the close of this journal,
I find it hard to tell you in words that are fitting
the last great event of my life.

Although, as I have said, Mr Fairfax was away in
London for a great length of time, he did pay us
a few flying visits at Solcombe; but did not bring
his wife with him, although Miss Fairfax had become
reconciled to the marriage, and all difference between
them was at an end. Indeed, although she was of
a somewhat quick temper, she was very fond of
her brother, and he of her; and latterly, had often
said to me that her brother did right, after all, in
marrying the woman he loved. It was all the more
to her credit that she had quite forgiven her brother's
marriage, for although she declares that it is not
true, and that she had no desire to marry, yet both
her brother and myself sometimes thought that she
was over-sensitive about it, and for that reason refused

many handsome offers she received from the gentlemen who from time to time she became acquainted with.

On one of these visits to Solcombe, Mr Fairfax
astonished me even more than he had done when
he introduced me to his wife. He had come over
to my farm to spend the evening, and we were
chatting over old times and having a glass of grog
together, when suddenly he opened upon me in this
way,—'Look here, Dew, I have always known you
to be pretty much of a fool, and I'll be hanged if
I don't think as you grow older you grow worse.
Here you are leading this miserable, lonely life, and
the woman who is willing to marry you is doing
the same, and so you go on month after month.
Meanwhile, the years are passing by, and by the
time you wake up to the fact (unless she proposes,
I don't believe you ever will), the pair of you will
be too old to make it worth while your mating.'

'Why, what on earth are you driving at, sir?'
I asked. Even up to this time I could not help
addressing the lieutenant as 'sir.'

'If you were anything but a fool you would know
that she can't ask you to marry her, yet she has
given you every signal that a woman in love can
make. She asks your advice on every subject, whether
you know anything of it or not, and I know—for
you have told me in your letters—that she is always
descanting to you on the mistake she made in once
supposing that it was wrong for two persons to

marry if they did not both happen to be born in the one station.'

'Great heavens, sir! you don't suppose that I could ever so far forget myself as to—to think of marrying with your sister!'

'Whenever are you going to forget that infernal humility that, since two or three years of service in the Marines, has so persistently stuck to you?'

'But, sir, our positions, apart from that, are widely different, and your sister, if she knew we were thus discussing her, would forbid me to speak to her again.'

'In the first place, our positions are not different. You are one of the most prosperous tenant farmers about here; and your father and his father came of good yeoman stock. I have an estate from which I derive a very moderate income, and my sister is dependent on what I allow her.'

'But, sir—'

'Wait a moment. In the second place, I have told her that you are very much in love with her, as I saw long ago, and she has confessed to me that if you would only get over your confounded modesty, you would not be indifferent to her. Now, sir, what have you to say to that?'

'But, sir, though I confess I have for a long time secretly admired Miss Charlotte, I have been most careful to conceal my sentiments, knowing too well my duty, and besides, notwithstanding all you say,

I can never, pardon me for saying it, believe Miss Fairfax thinks of me.'

'That will do, Dew ; put on your hat and coat this instant.'

And then before I realised what was to happen, he had marched me up to the Manor House, walked me straight into the drawing-room, where Miss Fairfax was sitting up for him, and then in the coolest manner in the world he said to her,—

'Charlotte, I have brought Will Dew up to see you. He has an important question to put to you, having first asked my permission, which I gave him with all my heart, and now I give the pair of you my blessing.'

With that he shoved me into the room, saying in a whisper, 'Go in and win, you confounded stupid,' and then went out and shut the door behind him, leaving me standing all confusion in the middle of the room. But when I saw the dear lady's sweet face so covered with blushes, my courage came and -- well, my children, I soon found my tongue too.

I have little else to tell you. We were married in old Solcombe church soon afterwards, and you children were born to us. What our lives have since been you well know, but this story of the early life of your father and his dearest friends you had only heard in scraps and patches from myself and your mother and your Uncle Fairfax. Now you know it all. Profit by the knowledge, and if you would learn the moral of my story, go back to the first page of my diary, and there read why I have set these things down in writing.

POSTSCRIPT

LET me re-open this journal and set down a few lines telling of the last years of those men whose brave hearts and wise heads so well and truly laid the foundation of the new world across the seas.

Our good and gallant Governor, Captain Phillip, before he died became an admiral, and up to the day of his death, in the year 1814, was dearly loved by all of those about him. In 1808 his old friend and comrade King, well worthy to be associated with such a man as Philip, met the Admiral at Bath, and from that place, only a week before his death, King wrote this letter to his son :—

'As this letter may reach you before you sail, I write to say that I came here merely to see Admiral Phillip, who I found much better than I could expect from the reports I had read, although he is quite a cripple, having lost the entire use of his right side ; but his intellects are very good, and his spirits are what they always were.'

Your Uncle Fairfax, too, with your mother, had the honour of again meeting his old commander during a brief visit that the Admiral made to Portsmouth, where he had gone at the desire of the Lords of the Admiralty to look at a new King's ship. At this time your Uncle Fairfax and your Aunt Mary were also staying at Portsmouth, and your mother, at their desire, went over to stay with them a week or two. It so happened that your Uncle Fairfax, hearing that the Admiral was staying at the house of a Gentleman whom he knew, went to see him and took your mother with him, though she remained outside in the carriage. Admiral Phillip was greatly pleased to see his former comrade, and showed that he had the warmest concern in all those who had served under him. Then, too, he even asked Mr Fairfax what had become of me, and when your uncle told him that I was well and prosperous, the old gentleman was pleased to say that I was a very careful man and would have made a good sailor, and so, when your uncle told him that I had married Miss Fairfax, his sister, and that Mrs Dew was then outside in the carriage, the gallant old officer, putting on his laced hat and leaning on your uncle's arm, came out to her and paid her many pretty compliments, saying, among other things, that Lieutenant King thought very highly of my conduct when the *Sirius* was wrecked at Norfolk Island. Before he bade them farewell he, taking a very handsome seal and chain from his fob, desired her to present it to me, 'as a

memento ' — these were his very words — ' of the
service we had seen together.' I need not tell you
how dearly I prize this gift, which you see I now
wear.

Of gallant, kind-hearted Hunter I have little to
tell, except that, soon after his return to England in
1801, he was appointed to the *Venerable*, seventy-
four, and when cruising off Torbay got his ship
ashore and wrecked in trying to save the life of a
man who had fallen overboard. He was tried by
court martial and acquitted, and in the course of
the trial was asked why he had put his ship about
in such a dangerous place. He replied, ' I consider the life of a British seaman of more value than
any ship in His Majesty's Navy.' Although by
such an answer he showed himself more kindly-
hearted than worldly - wise, he was afterwards promoted to be Rear-Admiral.

And by such men as these were the settlers in
the early days of New South Wales governed, and
when you hear people, as is often the case now-a-
days, saying that the prisoners were cruelly treated,
just take this journal of mine and read this post-
script to them, that all may know what manner of
men they were who founded New South Wales.

THE END

Colston & Company Ltd., Printers, Edinburgh.

www.ingramcontent.com/pod-product-compliance
Lightning Source LLC
Chambersburg PA
CBHW020856020726
47497CB00005B/1430